Tales From Between: 2 PBK D2D

A Strange Literary Journal

Elin Olausson, Ivy Grimes , Matthew Stott, Belicia Rhea, James Bennett, Katie McIvor, Briana Morgan

TALES FROM BETWEEN

London

www.talesfrombetween.wordpress.com

Copyright © 2023 by Tales From Between

All rights reserved.

Cover Design by Matthew Stott.

More To Read

Contents

Between You and Me   VII

Art   IX

1. Page Sixty-Seven   1
   by Belicia Rhea

2. Glass Cabbage   7
   by Ivy Grimes

3. Lilies   17
   by Elin Olausson

Art   33

4. If All Your Friends Jumped Off a Bridge   35
   by Katie McIvor

5. When the Guillotine Came   43
   by Matthew Stott

6. Avalanche   53
   by Briana Morgan

Art   59

7. The Cicatrix   61
   by James Bennett

Afterword   101

Art   103

More To Read   104

Between You and Me

Hello and welcome to *Tales From Between*. Each issue of this journal features a gathering of the fantastical and the horrific. Improbable stories written by a range of different authors, from the up-and-coming, to the established, to the never-heard-of-them.

We like strange stories. We hope you do, too. On you go then, *Strangers*, read well...
Matthew Stott

Support us on Patreon and help us continue to publish strange stories!

patreon.com/TalesFromBetween

TWITTER: @from_between | **INSTAGRAM:** @tales_from_between

Page Sixty-Seven

by Belicia Rhea

I heard my neighbor pacing along the sidewalk, whistling loud in the middle of the night. It sounded familiar, nearly operatic, and made something godawful stir inside of me. I couldn't figure out what he was doing, so I finally opened the window and asked if anything was wrong. He didn't answer. Just kept clapping his boots against the concrete. More whistling.

My fingers shook as I dug Q-tips into my ears, trying to scoop out that sound. I slammed the window shut and swallowed a few gulps of Benadryl, forced myself to sleep. Sister Elizabeth Grace sang in my dream and she looked exactly how she always did with those deep grooves of her wrinkles dented around her sunken black eyes, that hoarse and commanding voice louder than anyone's in the choir. The air filled with her rasping, and the congregation stared at her, trapped in endless rows of wooden pews.

Their faces blurred as I awoke to slivers of sun through my blinds. My neighbor was gone. But Sister Elizabeth Grace's voice still crawled in my ears. I thought of how the sisters used to circle around desks, how they'd strike me with rulers, make me memorize pages of Psalms. Each morning I'd recite my verses, bent down and anxious to keep the pleats sharp in my skirt—my knees raw in prayer, the hard floor thinning my pantyhose. Those days still linger, fused to me in memory.

I forced myself out of bed to check the mail, but the shakes didn't go. When I opened my mailbox, my key scratched the metal.

Inside lay a paper that read *God Bless You*, placed on top of a hymnal. I turned, and the mailman's face looked plastered on, unusual, and I couldn't help but feel like he'd heard the whistling, like he knew it too.

He looked at me, smiled, and said those three little words, like he was reading the paper out loud.

"God bless you," he said, as he held up a stack of the papers and hymnals, then continued loading them in other waiting boxes.

I heard the whistle again from somewhere near his truck. He kept his back to me as groups of people came over to us. All the neighbors seemed off. A few started humming, wagging their friendly waves with smiles cracking wide. I clapped my hands to my ears as I ran down our street, trying to drown out the noise.

Birds sang the first verse and the chorus began to whine from what sounded like a dog's howl near the north edge of Carthance and Roosevelt, the last turn before my house. I passed the street sign and looked down over the yellowed grass hill, but I couldn't find a dog. There was only a mother I'd never seen before, pushing a baby stroller and whispering music at the swaddle inside. I rushed for home, head pounding, running so fast I tripped and fell on my knees.

The scrapes on my palms were bleeding but I didn't care because everything was too loud, so I got in my car and drove. I wanted to escape, get some distance. It would be hard to follow me through these trees, stoplights, houses, gas stations, the turn into the shopping center. I parked and wandered through the empty lot, stopped to listen, but heard nothing—and walked toward the entrance to a grocery store.

Just past the sliding doors, a man started following me, and he was whistling too. He inched closer with each step, feet stomping down the aisle in a near march while the repetitions of light sliced lines in the ground as it caught the slick floor tiles. I went dizzy with each note stirring in his mouth, that song spewing all over like an infection. I knew it from the old days of Mass, sounded just like the Salve Regina.

"Hail, Holy Queen," a small voice began to sing, too sharp.

The voice belonged to a little girl with brown curls just like mine. She was over by the produce section, twirling around, swishing her pleated skirt. A gold cross necklace gleamed from her neck, and I remembered how my hair would get stuck in the clasp, tangled against that white collar of my school uniform.

I saw a nun turn the aisle corner, her lips moving. I squinted at her, thinking surely it couldn't be. I looked around and more people were singing, every face, and then the entire store began, but it sounded like the whole world.

Children skipped through the entrance, contorting their hands to show everyone the church steeples and finger people inside. Adults rounded their instrument mouths. They scraped the song out in their creaking baritones like a dying growl, out of breath and off key, licking the edges of their fingers to turn to page sixty-seven in their hymnals. Notes echoed off the ceiling slats with the hum of the industrial lights droning on like an organ, sound stretching large and hollow.

I felt her come up behind me—Sister Elizabeth Grace. That billowing black habit swept against my crossbody bag as her palms covered my mouth, squishing my lips open like a fish, her voice slithering down my neck as she shoved her hand inside the back of my throat, digging around for that whistle stuffed up inside of me, refusing to come out.

AUTHOR BIO

Belicia Rhea writes horror, weird fiction, and poetry. You can find her at beliciarhea.com and read more of her work published in Nightmare Magazine, Ligeia Magazine, and various anthologies. Her debut novella *Voracious* (June 2024) is forthcoming with Dark Matter INK.

Glass Cabbage

by Ivy Grimes

The old man and old woman were almost out of food. Salespeople sometimes took the path through the woods and dropped by their house to sell things like flour and oil and manufactured sweets, which supplemented their diet of eggs and vegetables and the occasional squirrel or rabbit. But their chickens and ripening vegetables had disappeared one night, and it had been weeks since a salesman from town had passed by.

"Maybe it was an animal who ate our vegetables," the old man said and they discussed the possibilities.

"Then who stole our chickens? Must have been a person. Pen's not damaged. No blood around."

The old man looked at the empty pen and wiped away a tear. "I reckon something bad happened in town. It's what we've always predicted."

"But we don't smell smoke, and we haven't heard anything that sounds like disaster."

"It might have happened in a different way than we thought it would."

The woods were quieter than usual.

"I'll have to try again to find a squirrel," the old man said, though he hated to shoot them.

"I'll do some foraging," the old woman said, and they went their separate ways.

She made a final inspection of their vegetable garden for any overlooked scraps, and she found a wilting carrot top lying on the ground, so she tossed it into her sack. There had to be something deeper in the woods, some source of food. She was sure she'd die if she didn't find something soon.

Winter was threatening, and the birds had eaten all the blackberries. Under the tallest oak trees in the forest, she found a couple of mushrooms for her bag. Nothing else. She kept going until she was somewhere she didn't recognize. A thick row of thorn bushes seemed to have been placed specifically in her way, keeping her from something, so she pushed through them and ignored the pricks to her arms and face. On the other side, there was a field. A field! She didn't know there were any farmers in the middle of the woods.

"Don't get excited," she reminded herself. When things were bad, they usually got worse. Naturally, the field was plucked bare. Since she didn't notice anyone around, she decided to look around to see if any bit of food was overlooked.

Inside a dug-up row, she found a tiny potato. Into the bag it went. Was that all? No, there was something else there, at the far end of the field. A beautiful large leaf hid (she knew) something ripe and edible. She ran to the thick leaf and lifted it like a veil, and underneath she found a hard thing that glinted in the afternoon sun. It was a huge cabbage made of green-tinted glass.

"A glass cabbage." She held it up to her face and whispered to it. Its surface was foggy with dew, but when she wiped it with her shirt, she saw something inside. A big toe. A rather large big toe.

She wished that the toe was a doll and that the toenail was the doll's face. It was hard to accept what it was. The severed bottom of the toe was neatly bandaged, at least, and the toenail was well-cared for. When she turned the glass cabbage, rolling it around to see the toe from different angles, the toe moved, too. It bumped against the glass edges in a way that looked painful. But there was no one to feel any pain from it, was there?

So freshly preserved, that toe was. Pale pink, like a healthy pig. Any piece of meat could be prepared. It would be like skinning a squirrel.

She couldn't fit the glass cabbage in her bag. It would have torn the seams. So she took up the cabbage in both arms and carried it home, needlessly shielding the glass from thorns. She couldn't stop staring at the big toe inside. It must have been the toe of a giant. Distracted, she didn't see a thick tangle of roots at her feet. She tripped, and the glass cabbage flew into the air. Before she could catch it, it fell on the hard roots and shattered.

She wanted to cry, but she stood up and picked her way through the broken glass to get to the toe. It was frightening to pick it up with her bare hands, but she was desperate. She picked it up by its bandage and gave it a quick sniff. It had the same metallic smell as meat.

"It's a sign," she said to herself. She would have had to smash the glass cabbage to get at the big toe anyway. "Fresh meat."

She rushed along, feeling like she was in some kind of danger until she reached her backyard. There, she prepared the toe. She half-ignored what she was doing, knowing she couldn't relish her meal as much if she thought about the discarded parts. This was even easier than a squirrel in one sense. No guts. She used her ax to remove the toenail, and she peeled away the bandage, and she tried not to look at the toe before she dropped it in her boiling pot of water. She quickly dug a hole to bury the toenail and the bandage.

She put the measly carrot top and mushrooms and the tiny potato that she'd found into the pot, and she used some salt from her cupboard. After some time, the smell was intoxicating, and she looked into the pot and saw that the skin was beginning to separate from the meat. She pulled it off with metal tongs and dug a quick hole to bury the skin. She hated to waste any part of the meat, but there was something disturbing about that skin. It had the faded labyrinth of a toe print on it. Had it been another animal's skin, she would have eaten it.

When the thing was cooked, it looked so tender. She used her tongs to shred the meat, and finally, she removed the bone from the stew and put it into another hole she'd dug. Soon, the remnants of the toe were buried in three different spots in her yard, and she had a delicious stew in her pot. She used her ladle to give it a taste, and it tasted no different from pork stew. Maybe it was even better.

She kept tasting, waiting for the old man to return. If the stew kept cooking, the meat would get tough. Finally, she decided to ladle herself a bowlful.

He was far away, no doubt, trying to set a slow trap for some creature. It was annoying of him not to know when to give up.

As she was eating the stew, she was disturbed a time or two by memories of finding the big toe and preparing it for the pot. It made her shiver to remember what it had been. Thinking about the buried remnants upset her, too. It was like she'd killed a man and buried his corpse in her yard.

No, no, nothing to worry about. The toe was meant for her. It had been placed there in that glass cabbage (which must have been some kind of magic), and it was like it had called her name. She had known just where to go to find it.

She hadn't eaten so well in years. The salesmen were willing to trade with them, to accept eggs for their goods, but the old woman suspected they were taking pity on them. When she was hungry, she hadn't cared, but now that she was almost full, she was beginning to feel ashamed. Anyone who lived in town must have found them awfully pitiful. Maybe the old man liked being an object of pity because it made him interesting, and he liked to talk to the salesmen who wandered by and tell them stories of life in the woods, but the old woman didn't like it. She saw herself as strong and happy, and the old man seemed to see her that way too. It confused her when others didn't see her the same way, and it made her ask herself unhelpful questions. What was so great about being from one of the towns?

She kept eating. Her stomach raged for the stew, for every drop of it. When she was finished, she even used her fingers to scoop out the bits of carrot top stuck to the walls of the pot, and she savored the bits of grease that clung to the greens.

While she ate, she kept thinking the old man would catch her red-handed. But he didn't. By the time he came home, it was pure night, and the pot had already been scrubbed and the fire put out. She was in bed when she heard him open the door. She pretended to be asleep when he came into the bedroom and took off his clothes and lay down beside her.

"I can smell it outside. You found something. You didn't wait for me," he said.

"What do you think about that?" she said without opening her eyes.

"I was trying too hard to find what wasn't there. But you still should have saved me something. Some scrap of something." He didn't sound angry or even sad. He sounded like his feelings had floated away, up into the night sky.

"I did it for a reason, but I don't know what the reason is," she said. "I was so hungry. I think my body knows something."

"You want me to die?" he said.

"No. I just want to live."

The toe was meant for her. It thundered in her body as she digested it. It could have been an evil toe, but it was hers. The old man might have gotten sick when he realized what he was eating, which would have ruined the meal.

They couldn't make sense of it, either together or separately. Without meaning to, the old woman fell asleep. Some time later, a voice in the distance woke her up.

"Who?" That was all she heard at first. "Who?"

"It's someone from the town," she said to herself. "They're having a disaster. But I'm not going out there."

The voice was still distant, but it seemed to draw closer. "Who? Who? Who stole?"

"I didn't steal," she said aloud, sitting up in bed. The old man snored beside her.

"Who stole my big toe?" The voice was like a whistling wind prefiguring a tornado or terrible hail.

"I didn't steal it! You left it there!"

In spite of her protests, she found herself running through the darkness to look outside for the source of the voice. The night was clear and cold. Must have been a bad dream.

No, there it was again. "Who stole?" It sounded like a person had been trapped in a cloud or the moon and was trying to speak through it. Whatever it was, the creature was getting closer.

"Show yourself! If you're going to accuse me, then do it to my face. I won't be afraid of a possibility. You set me up to fail. I was hungry, and you put your toe out there, and you expected me not to eat it? It was calling to me!"

"You stole my big toe!" the voice said, but it was quieter than before.

"The choice you gave me wasn't fair." She felt ashamed for her complaints, like she was a child whining to her parents. But this was life or death. It was the difference between guilt or innocence.

She waited for the voice to accuse her again, but it didn't.

AUTHOR BIO

Ivy Grimes is here, and her stories have appeared in The Baffler, ergot., Seize the Press, Vastarien, Tales From Between, and elsewhere. Sign up for her occasional thoughts and author interviews at ivygrimes.substack.com.

Lilies

by Elin Olausson

The cottage didn't look like it had in the pictures, but Lo was tired and needed to sleep. She unpacked the toothbrushes and the pastel bedsheets while the fire crackled and Dan hummed a tune she couldn't quite place, but knew she didn't like. The wind ghosted outside the windows, slipping in here and there, breathing ice. The view was all woods and darkness, and she wished there had been shutters. It wasn't until they were in bed, huddled close together for warmth, that she inhaled Dan's sweat and asked him if they'd made a mistake.

"Don't worry, kitten." He had always called her that and it made her feel safe, like being tucked in a blanket. "You didn't like it much in town, remember? All those kids. Here, you'll be able to focus on just the one."

Dan was right. She hadn't liked the crowded suburban school with its littered hallways and savage eight-year-olds. Her new workplace was a much better fit, and instead of handling an entire class she'd be in charge of a young girl who needed special assistance. She'd make a difference for someone, and she wouldn't have to lock herself in the bathroom crying every day.

"Won't you be bored when I'm at work?" she asked, tracing the hair on his chest with her fingers. The hairs were coarse but shone like gold.

"No. I'll sleep in and then read books in bed, and when you come home we can talk about your day."

"Yes. Okay."

"Now sleep, all right? You don't want to be late tomorrow." His chest rose and fell, rose and fell, and she pushed her face into it, the next day already whispering in her ear. Its voice tinkled like a silver bell.

The village was a five-minute drive away. It popped up from nowhere, a cluster of low wooden houses leaning on each other. A Rottweiler sat on a porch, but when she drove past it ran up to the fence, barking. The sound filled the car, drilled into her brain, and she had a glimpse of the dog's eyes looking straight at her. They were a sick, muddy color, like milk tea.

There were no other cars parked outside the school, which was red and wooden and made her think of white-aproned girls. She went inside, breathing chalky air, listening to the echo of her own feet. The principal's office was the third door from the entrance, and she knocked and waited.

The door opened and an old woman peered at her. It was too dusky inside to make out what her face looked like, but her hair was spun-glass brittle and gray. The hand resting on the door had long nails, yellowed around the edges.

"Lo Linde? Come inside. I've made us coffee."

The office was crammed, bookshelves covering the walls and a third of the only window. Lo pretended to sip the coffee and avoided looking at the principal's nails.

"Well, it's nice to meet you. I'm Kerstin Wik, but of course you know that already." She grinned. Her teeth were yellow, too. "There are some forms to fill in, but you can do that later and hand them to me by the end of the day. I'm sure what you're most interested in right now is to meet Nora."

The girl's name was Nora. Dan's grandmother had had that name and Lo looked forward to telling him about it. He would smile and say something clever, and his fingers would sift through her hair.

"It's fortunate that you could start so soon," Kerstin said, covering the coffee mug with her hand. Her nails tapped against the ceramic, long, dirty. "Nora's been struggling ever since she first started school, but we haven't felt the need to bring in a support teacher until now. During last term she refused to come to school, refused to talk, everything. We hope this solution will work out for her. She is here today, at least, waiting for you at the end of the hall."

Lo nodded, the smell of coffee nauseating.

"Take this day just to get to know her, gain her trust." Kerstin pushed the stack of forms toward her, sheets of paper cluttered with tiny black print. "You and I can discuss the details tomorrow."

When Lo came back out into the hallway it was as quiet and empty as before, her footsteps slamming against the linoleum. There were doors on both sides, a staircase, and rows of empty hangers. The walls were painted white like in institutions, hospitals.

At the end of the hall there was one final door, gray like the others. Lo opened it and saw a table, an empty chair, a girl. The girl was tall for her age but wore a blouse with a childish print. She had her hair in tight pigtails and her lips looked swollen, as if she had chewed them raw.

Lo closed the door and sat down opposite Nora, who watched her without saying anything. The round glasses made her eyes appear larger than they were.

"Hi. I'm Lo." Lo put the forms down in front of her and glanced at the first page. The words threw themselves at her—*address, date of birth, next of kin*—and she turned the page, the paper slicing her finger open.

"You don't have to tell me your name. I know a little bit about you already. You're called Nora and you're twelve, aren't you?"

Nora opened her mouth but didn't say anything. Lo turned her head to get a view of the claustrophobic room. It was windowless and glum, with a low bookshelf in the corner, books heaped haphazardly on top of each other. Even from a distance, it was obvious that they were many decades old.

"Let me tell you about myself, then. I just moved here with Dan; that's my boyfriend. We lived in the city before but we always wanted to get closer to nature."

Nora's eyes turned toward the door. Her face was smooth and small but in that moment she looked ancient, and it made something inside Lo squirm.

"Why would you move here?" Nora asked, her voice a silver bell, and Lo realized that there was nothing wrong with her.

"What was it that made you refuse to come to school?"

The silence twisted between them, foggy like the eyes of the Rottweiler. Nora picked at a hole in the shoulder seam of her blouse, head hanging.

"You'll see why," she said. Lo wanted to keep asking but still not—the thought of the barking dog had unnerved her, and her brain glued Nora's words to its fangs, its evident madness. She went over to the shelf, grabbed a book at random and put it in front of Nora on the table.

"I need to find out at what level you are. What about this, is it familiar?"

Nora watched the pages, her face stiff, statue-like. Lo followed her gaze and saw that the book was illustrated. The picture that filled the right page showed a man with his eyes gouged out, staring blindly ahead with blood running down his cheeks.

"What's this doing here?" She snatched the book away, studying the spine and the cover. *Grimms' Fairy Tales*. The cover was innocent; gilded letters on a bottle green background, just another vintage book of fairy tales.

"Those stories are much gorier than people think," Nora said, still staring at the spot where the book had been. "The witch found out that the prince had been seeing Rapunzel, so she punished him by making him blind."

"You know it, then." Lo put the book away, briefly scanning the other titles on the shelf. Well-used textbooks, English and History and Math. Thirty years old, perhaps thirty-five, forty. Was it just Nora who had to make do with them, or did the other pupils use the same books?

Nora turned her eyes to the bare white wall. "Sometimes when they tell me to read I make it look like I'm reading, but I'm shutting my eyes off. Thinking thoughts that are all mine."

Lo wondered what Dan was doing. The air in the crammed room was sour and she breathed in small, calculated puffs. "I'll bring you notebooks," she said. "For your thoughts."

The cottage seemed deserted when she came home and for a moment a scream grew inside her, but it faded when Dan appeared in the bedroom doorway. His hair was tousled and there was a twinkle in his eyes that spoke of languid, bright-colored dreams.

"Welcome back, kitten. How was your day?"

Lo melted in his arms, became shapeless and fluid. "I think I'll get along well with the girl." She didn't tell him about Kerstin Wik and her long nails, the row of unused hangers in the hallway, or the barking dog.

"Of course you will." Dan kissed her above the left eyebrow. Before they'd met she hadn't liked anything about her face, but he had made her hate it less.

"I told Nora I'd get her a notebook," she said, then realized the name had to be kept confidential. But who would Dan tell?

"Wait here." Dan let go of her and went into the bedroom, then came back with a blue notebook she vaguely remembered. "Give her this. I never use it anyway."

Lo didn't want him to give his things away, but it wasn't as if there were any nearby bookstores. The school had writing material for the pupils, she supposed, cupboards crammed with cheap, concrete gray stationery and flimsy lined paper. But she wanted to give Nora a thing from outside, a thing the principal didn't know about.

"Thank you." She took the book, pressing it to her chest. Dan leaned against her and started humming. It was that tune, the one she didn't like, and she tried telling him to stop but couldn't. When she closed her eyes she saw Nora in front of her, sitting at the table in that tiny room. As if she was always there, waiting.

———

The Rottweiler rushed to the gate the next morning as well, mad barks tearing into her skin. She wondered if it hated all cars or just hers, but there was no one else driving by so she couldn't find out. The schoolyard was as empty as it had been yesterday, swings hanging limp, the slide dappled with rust. At the school in the city there had always been children playing outside, their shrieks headache-inducing, feral. She had been on painkillers every day, maximum dosage, her purse laden with medication. Here, she had only Nora to care about.

She was on the porch stairs when she discovered the man crouched by the flowerbed below the window. An aged man, shriveled, in a ratty knitted sweater and muddy rubber boots.

"Who are you?"

The man lifted his head slowly. His gray hair was thick, fur-like, but his face sagged like a dry plum. There was a grin lurking in the corners of that face, a grin that made her think of those painkiller days and all the rowdy children.

"Just the janitor," he said, pointing a grimy finger at his chest. His nails were long and filthy.

"Oh." Lo kept her eyes on that finger, her insides coiling.

"You ask me if you need anything, Lo Linde. Anything at all." He nodded his shaggy head once before resuming work. Lo slipped into the building, the remnants of the man's raspy voice sticking to her. *He's not a real janitor. He's something else.*

She was hurrying toward the room where Nora waited when Kerstin stepped out of her office and blocked the way. Her thin hair clouded on top of her head like a halo, and she wore red lipstick that had stained her front teeth.

"Lo! We have an appointment, remember?"

No, Lo didn't remember. She didn't want to sit opposite Kerstin and discuss the curriculum, but she did it because it was required of her. Kerstin handed her documents, opened binders, talked. Lo watched her teeth, red and yellow like the fall, and she forced herself not to think about nails.

Nora sat in the room waiting when she dashed inside hours later, shutting the door. She was in the same blouse as yesterday and looked even younger, as if she had shrunk.

"This is yours." Lo handed her the blue notebook and Nora opened it slowly, peering inside.

"There's a name in it," she said. "Daniel."

Lo arranged her face neatly, like a set table. "Don't worry about that."

"Thank you." Nora put the book aside. Her pigtails were long enough to brush against the table when she moved. "Our cat just had a litter of kittens. I'll write down their names and their birthday."

"Good." For a moment Lo was floundering, lost. Then she went up to the blackboard and started writing numbers, and she talked, and at three o'clock the school day was over and she drove home, keeping her eyes away from the village houses. Dan fell asleep quickly that night but she stayed awake, listening to the woods and the tiny creatures in the walls. She hummed quietly to ward them off but the tune she hated kept disturbing her, as if it was always hiding right beneath the surface. It smelled heavy, like decaying flowers.

The weekdays blended, her hands locking and unlocking the car, the dog clawing at the gate every time she passed. A shadow moved in the window once, fingers touching the curtain, eyes. Whoever was in there saw the dog, the road, the passing car, and Lo had no idea who they were.

Nora didn't seem to enjoy their classes, but she didn't stay away from school. Her hair was always neat but her clothes were worn, faded, washed too many times, and they smelled of mothballs and attic dust. Lo gave her assignments and mock exams, made her read aloud from the books on the shelf. Nora held them close to her face and dragged the words out of her chest at a slow, monotonous pace, as if they didn't matter. Whenever an unfamiliar word showed up her voice hitched, paused, and in that pause were other words that Lo put in her pocket to make sense of later. But whenever she tried to recall Nora's secret messages, all she heard was labored breathing.

At the end of each day, Lo leaned her forehead against the blackboard and told Nora to write in her notebook. "Write whatever you want. Whatever you think of." She had used to write stories of her own once. Before the words shriveled and died inside her.

Dan told her she did good. His skin was warm and she sank her nails into it, heaving deep dark breaths.

"There are mice in the walls," she said. "Haven't you heard?"

His face shifted and she realized that no, of course he hadn't heard.

"What do you want to do about it, kitten?"

Kitten. "I'm going to ask Nora. If I can have one."

Dan watched her as she put on her coat, scarf, boots. "It'll be dark soon. Do you even know where she lives?"

"I know the address. It's farther into the woods, apparently." She grabbed a flashlight, tested it. It showered the dusky hall in unnatural, silvery light, and she quickly switched it off.

"Good luck," Dan said. When she leaned against him she got a whiff of lilies.

Lo Linde had never been afraid of the woods. She was afraid of other things, things to do with people, but what harm could trees do? She walked fast, flashlight swinging, pine needles crunching under her soles. The cottage was a five-minute drive from the main road; she wouldn't bump into anyone. The woods hissed and writhed but she didn't mind. It couldn't hurt her, unlike the outside world.

She might have been lost if it weren't for the porch light outside Nora's house, leading her in the right direction. It reminded her of a movie she had once seen, a burning eye in the darkness, and she banished the unsettling image from her mind.

The house was tall and muddy gray, as if the wall paint had been washed off. The pines lurked by the windows, twigs and branches hanging over the porch's wooden fence. Lo couldn't see a car, and there were no lights on except for the bulb illuminating the porch.

She knocked hard. It was only a few moments until the door opened and Nora stood there, barefoot and thin in a striped nightshirt. The hallway behind her was dusky, and she carried with her a sour scent Lo couldn't place.

"So this is your home."

Nora didn't answer. Her fingers squeezed the door handle and her eyes darted to it every now and then.

"I came about the kittens," Lo said. "You said you've got some."

Shadows darkened Nora's face. "Not anymore."

Lo tried to look past her shoulder, into the house. "Are your parents in?"

Nora lowered her voice until it was barely a voice at all. "I live with my grandparents."

"Oh." It was strange that the principal hadn't mentioned it. For such a young girl to live without her parents, something bad must have happened.

"You really have to go now." Nora jerked her head to the side, as if someone had called her name. Lo thought she heard something—a croaky hiss from the unlit rooms inside. She supposed a decent teacher would have demanded to have been let in, but all the right words were glued to the roof of her mouth, useless. Nora shut the door and Lo left, back through the woods, flashlight leading the way. When she came home the mice scratched and chewed, and Dan hummed louder than ever.

Neither of them mentioned the house call in school the next morning. Nora sat with her back straight, reading out loud, writing in the notebook. The building pressed against Lo's temples, too large and too quiet, like a tomb. The hallway's empty hangers bothered her, and to ward them off she asked Nora to sing, sing whatever she wanted. Nora put her hands in her lap and sang Christmas carols though it wasn't winter, the tiny room bursting with her silver bell voice.

"Keep at it," Lo said, thinking less about hangers and more about snow. Nora paused for a moment and then started singing hymns. Lo recognized the high-pitched tunes, the archaic wording. Would Kerstin Wik be able to hear? Would she be angry that Lo had found a way to break the system, whatever the system was?

Another hymn flowed from Nora's lips—a hymn that reeked of lilies, church candles, and coffin wood. Lo reached over the table and clasped a hand over her mouth, nails scratching the girl's skin.

"Not that one!" She could shut Nora up, but she was never able to ask Dan to stop humming it. There was something in the way, always something.

Nora stared at her, breathing hard. She was only a child, and they hadn't even let her keep one kitten.

"I'm sorry. I'm sorry." Lo combed her fingers through her hair. It was shorter than she remembered. "Go out and play. It's breaktime."

Once Nora had left, she picked up the blue notebook. She tore open the first page and read. Nora's handwriting was neat like an old lady's, and she had no spelling mistakes.

She scares me, the book said. *I don't want to be here*. There were other passages, webbing across the pages, blending into something foul. Lo read but her eyes kept shifting focus, the words hiding behind each other. *She. Scares. Me*. Was it the grandmother—that hissing voice in the darkness? Or the principal? Nora had seemed frightened in her own home, a crumbling child in the doorway. Something was wrong in the village; something had always been wrong. The Rottweiler, its mad eyes. The empty hangers. It had something to do with Kerstin Wik, with the leering janitor. Their long and filthy nails. Lo shouldn't have come here, she shouldn't have brought Dan to a place like this. She needed to leave before they found out she knew. Before they tried to stop her.

Standing, she went over to the bookshelf and tore the books down. They rained to the floor, backs splitting, pages dancing like flakes of snow. The book of fairy tales landed on top and the prince grinned at her, the blinded prince, blood on his face and he looked like Dan, exactly like Dan, and she needed to get home before it was too late.

She walked through the hallway one last time, the hangers tittering behind her back. Kerstin Wik's door was closed and Lo wondered if she was in there, if the janitor was in there, if they were one and the same. In the schoolyard she found Nora by the fence, arms hanging.

"Come on. We're going."

"What?" Nora stared at her. "Why?"

"You can leave some hours early. I'll drive you home." She put her hand on Nora's shoulder and steered her toward the car, the only car in the parking lot, the only car in the world.

"No, that's okay." Nora tried to shrug her hand off but Lo wouldn't let her.

"Don't fuss now, just get in the car." She opened the passenger door and shoved the girl inside. Sat down in the driving seat and started the engine.

"My grandparents will be worried," Nora said. There was a new hitch in her voice, the sound of something collapsing.

"Everything will be all right." Lo drove past the dog house at high speed but couldn't hear the barking now that Nora was with her. "We'll just pick up my boyfriend, and then we'll get away from here."

Nora started crying. It was ugly and embarrassing, but Lo didn't know how to make it stop. The woods swallowed them and when she thought about seeing Dan her chest fluttered like fizzy drinks and a swarm of moths. "You'll really like him," she said. "He's the kindest person there is."

"Just let me go," Nora sobbed. "I won't tell anyone."

The cottage stood there just as she had left it, low, single storey. Nora didn't want to follow her inside but Lo made her, so that the girl wouldn't run away. Dan could keep an eye on her while Lo packed.

"Sweetie? I brought a friend home."

Dan came into the hallway and frowned at her. His hair was messy and long, and she never grew tired of looking at him.

"What have you done now?" he asked. He smelled wrong, of lilies, of coffin wood.

"The right thing," Lo said and pushed Nora hard, because Nora was making too much noise. She stared at Lo as the mice came through the walls and Dan started singing the funeral hymn, his voice like a silver bell.

"Who are you talking to?" Nora screamed. "There's no one there!"

Lo looked at Dan so that he would make it stop, make it go back to how it was before. "He's right there. Right there. Right there." She grabbed him and the smell of lilies washed over her, rotting, dead. Something broke inside her head; something that had been whole once, back when he was still alive. She tore at warm skin and vaguely remembered that there had been a little girl once, and her name had been Nora. Then the memory slipped away and all that remained was Dan, his face, his voice that would never leave her.

You did well, kitten. You did so well.

AUTHOR BIO

Elin Olausson is a fan of the weird and the unsettling. She is the author of the short story collection *Growth* and has had stories featured in The Ghastling, Luna Station Quarterly, Nightscript, and many other publications. Elin's rural childhood made her love and fear the woods, and she firmly believes that a cat is your best companion in life. She lives in Sweden.

If All Your Friends Jumped Off a Bridge

by Katie McIvor

(CW: suicide)

It's a familiar question, one we've all heard. It's the one your mother used to ask when you got into trouble. An ugly, tiresome question. But perhaps it gains new meaning for you today.

You've never really thought about the bridge before. It's different once you're standing here, with the river far below, the wet-cold air stinging your eyes. You can smell watery rot, the whiff of dead things. There's darkness below the surface. Darkness and dirty water. And perhaps other things, too.

You left home this morning not knowing you'd end up at the bridge. That's not unusual – the bridge can surprise people – but it's also not *not* unusual, you understand. For most, the bridge looms up gradually. You might sense it from a young age, or after a difficult life event.

Its shadow might darken your horizon as you edge towards adulthood, always alert for the glare of sunlight on steel, the whine of wind between railings.

You don't talk to your friends about the bridge. If your friends end up there too, that's on them.

So you didn't know where you were going, this fine November afternoon. You walked in a pack, probably. A shrieking, schoolgirl pack, the kind that old ladies cross the street to avoid. You chewed gum, swapping headphones between the intimate, soft-skinned hollows of your ears.

So how did you end up at the bridge? Was it a dare, a stupid joke? *So-and-so or so-and-so's brother or sister did it here.* Did what? *You know what. Let's go look*, you probably said. You like to scare each other, at that age. (At any age.) *Let's go see where they jumped.*

You assumed the police would have installed a safety rail. Blocked off the footpath, even. All those deaths! There should be memorials, flowers, handmade signs taped into plastic to protect them from the rain. It should be a site of national mourning.

But it's not. It's just the same old bridge. You looked for yellow tape, for WARNING signs. STEEP DROP. DANGER. Seeing none, you crept closer. Onto the bridge itself. Hands on the railing, single file. Slowly, as if escorting a coffin.

In the middle of the bridge, you formed your neat little row, looking down. That's when you got the giggles. You yanked each other's arms, screaming, pretending to skid towards the edge. Thoughts of so-and-so's brother or sister evaporated in the face of your exhilaration. The water stared up at you, black and impassive.

I don't understand your laughter. I'm not like you any more.

My own experience blurs into itself the longer I'm down here. I don't remember individual incidents, only feelings. The scarlet embarrassment of being *different*. The way I looked down, always down, as though staring into deep water even then. The gut-sick loathing. The rage which pulsed with misery until rage and misery became one.

It got worse after puberty. Social capital began to translate into sexual value, which translates into self-worth. I stood at the mirror and squished my own face as if it were putty. Smeared the makeup I wasn't allowed around both eyes until I couldn't see myself any more. Tried to pretend I was pretty, although it wouldn't have helped. Even then, I saw the outline of the bridge, etched across my tearful, teenage eye like a floating lash.

So: to return to the railing. You're there, and you're cold (none of your friends wore a coat, so neither did you). The wind moves along the bridge with purpose, as though trying to push you back to firm ground. You ignore it. You're a fourteen-year-old girl; you can't be swayed.

Should we do it?

Your friends shuffle closer, giggling. This is a lark to them. Everything is – school, grades, family. They've got their whole lives ahead of them.

Beringed hands clamp the railing. The girls release high-pitched screams of laughter into the breeze. You're silent. Your throat has closed up.

So-and-so did it. So-and-so really jumped. Stood right here, and jumped.

From my chiaroscuro vantage below the surface, I watch your friends shriek and grip each other's hands, up there on the bridge. You're at the end of the line. Pretending to shriek too, your mouth wide, wondering if you belong there at all. You're not really going to jump, are you? Are they?

I never thought I'd do it, either. Nobody ever does. It's a game in your head until the last minute. A what-if, a why-not. But there were no friends to hold my hands that day.

They did a study once, of people who'd been to the bridge and survived. Not this particular bridge, but then this bridge isn't particular. Some bridges are, for our purposes – the Golden Gate; the Nanjing Yangtze River Bridge – but really it's every bridge, it's any bridge. The survivors all knew they would survive. They never doubted it.

If you jump off the Golden Gate Bridge, you're two hundred and fifty feet up. Two hundred and sixty, at low tide. You travel that distance at around seventy-five miles per hour.

Can you imagine the high?

Once you jump, for most people, it's game over. The water smacks into you with the force of a freight train. If not killed on impact, you drown. I don't remember which happened to me. What I remember is opening my eyes in the darkness of the below-bridge and seeing the riverbed, with its dank scattering of litter.

When you fall, I'll be waiting. The water is dark and cold like a chest full of guilt. Swim down towards me, my love. I'll take your bloated hands in mine. Together we'll swim, you and I and all of your friends who jumped with you. We'll be a shoal of smooth and limber corpses among the weeds and broken shopping trolleys of the riverbed.

Isn't it tempting?

So I ask you again, my dear, my darling: if all your friends jumped off a bridge – would you?

AUTHOR BIO

Katie McIvor is a Scottish writer and library assistant. Her short fiction has appeared or is forthcoming in magazines such as *The Deadlands*, *Interzone*, *Neon*, and *Three-Lobed Burning Eye*, and her three-story collection is out now with Ram Eye Press. You can find her on Twitter at @_McKatie_ or on her website at katiemcivor.com.

When the Guillotine Came

by Matthew Stott

The guillotine appeared without warning, straddling the town. Five times as tall as the largest building, it loomed, monstrous, the blade shimmering high at midnight like a second moon.

Laurie first saw it from her bedroom window, the fog of sleep dulling her senses. The house was too close to the structure to make sense of it, the dark wood bisecting her view, so she dismissed it at first, yawning and making her way downstairs for breakfast.

It was her grandfather, who rose a good hour before the rest of the house to take brisk early morning walks, that brought the guillotine properly to her attention.

"A what?" asked Laurie, who'd never heard the word used before.

"A guillotine. A tool of execution. You kneel, rest your neck against it, and down comes a heavy, sharp blade, separating your head from the rest of you. *Whack*!"

"That's barbaric!"

Her grandfather shrugged and dolloped a spoonful of blood red jam into the centre of his porridge.

Laurie and her parents left their breakfasts behind to go and see for themselves, only to find most of the town had done the same. Laurie wormed her way through the press of people until she reached the dark wood of the structure. She reached out and pressed her palm flat to its surface; the wood was damp, viscous, like touching a tongue.

"How big d'you reckon that blade is?" asked young Jackson Porter, her neighbour, squinting upwards. Porter was a year older than Laurie at sixteen, his chin starting to grow dark with stubble.

"Hard to tell," she replied.

"Big as a house, I'd say. At least."

Laurie wiped her hand against her dress, the palm still sticky from the wood.

Everyone at the town meeting had ideas about what should be done.

"We should cut it down!"

"Burn the thing!"

"Blow it up!"

But the truth was it was too large a job to be tackled safely. Any way they could think of to remove the giant interloper would surely have resulted in catastrophic damage to the surrounding buildings. It was agreed that the best thing was to just accept the presence of the guillotine, strange as it was. After all, it wasn't hurting anyone. Besides, it might draw tourists to the town, and tourists brought money.

"Where do you think it came from?" Laurie asked her family.

"Could be a trick of some sort," Dad said, tapping his rough chin with the stem of his pipe.

"What, d'you think a nearby town wheeled it in whilst we slept?" asked Grandfather, mocking his son-in-law. "It would take a thousand men, no, ten thousand men to drag that thing. And someone would've seen, or heard! No, one moment it wasn't there, and the next, it was. Simple as that."

"It's judgement," offered Grandma, sourly knitting a blanket, the bone white needles beating out a sharp, insistent pattern.

"Judgement from where?" asked Laurie.

"Heaven or Hell or elsewhere altogether, don't matter, it's judgement."

———

It's remarkable how quickly people can become accustomed to the strange. By the fifth day, the guillotine had slipped down the roster of things to talk about as the town grew used to its hulking presence. It was almost as though it had always been a part of the town. Some took to picnicking at the base of the enormous legs, leaning back against it, holding a loved one tight.

It was on the sixth night that the guillotine made itself heard for the first time.

The sound woke everyone that had already taken to their beds. It made some curl tight into a ball of dread in their damp, twisted blankets, and forced others to step out onto the street, to fall to the cobbles and gaze up at the shimmering blade with unblinking awe.

The guillotine was hungry.

It was hungry and it begged to be fed.

It did not do so with words, but a mournful, petulant cry that drilled its desire into the bones and meat of every resident in town.

"But it doesn't have a mouth, how can it make such sounds?" asked Mother to her perplexed husband.

"Best not to think about it, I expect," was his response.

Laurie found Grandma on her knees in the street.

"Come back inside," she said, but the old woman could not hear her, she only heard the cry of the guillotine.

As the sun rose, so the structure's voice quietened. People went about their days as best they could, but a fetid air of expectation blanketed the place. They now understood that the guillotine was no benign newcomer, but that there was a purpose to its arrival.

"We should make sure the house is secure at night," said Mother, and her husband agreed. He fixed wooden shutters over each window, a heavy padlock would keep them closed after dark. Laurie could see it gave her father some sense of calm to be actively preparing for what was to come.

During the day, the guillotine cast an enormous shadow, making the town a sundial, counting down the minutes until nightfall whereupon the structure would take up its despairing plea once more.

"Please stay inside tonight," said Laurie to her grandma.

"Don't you tell me what to do, you're not too old to bend over my knee," was the sharp response.

That night, Laurie again found her grandma in the street, gazing up at the giant as its desperate wail washed over the streets and the buildings. Its voice was a raging river that nothing could hold back, it penetrated each darkened alley, each filth spackled gutter, each fortified home. Laurie's grandfather had now joined his wife, his baggy, rheumy eyes wide with wonder.

At first the townspeople resisted the urge to sate the guillotine's gnawing hunger, but with each day that passed, the pleading grew more insistent, more pitiful. A bleating, pathetic call that rang out through the dark. Laurie, unable to sleep, walked the streets, the sound making her jaw tight, her breath short. She noticed that it was the town's oldest residents that seemed captivated by the cry. They were the ones on their knees in front of their homes, gazing up with veneration. They would be the first to comply with the monster's plea.

It was the end of the second week of the guillotine's presence that the feast began. One by one, the oldest people in town stepped into the sky, ready to feed the starving blade. They did not jump or climb, they simply began to step upwards, as though on some staircase that no one else could see. When they reached their destination, they would bow, resting their necks in the eager maw, smiles stretching their faces.

And so the blade would fall.

But the severed heads did not.

A fine mist of blood flecked the world below, but the heads, once free of their bodies, flew like birds, ecstatic, and circled in procession above the rooftops, singing songs of adoration to the guillotine.

In the morning, Laurie stood before her house, peering up at the heads that swam above. She tried to tell which one belonged to Grandma, to Grandfather, but there were too many and they were too high to know for sure.

"Don't," said Mother, "it's morbid."

"Someone should get a net and fetch them down," said Father, but notably did not go in search of any netting himself.

Laurie and her parents held a small ceremony, but had nothing to bury, nothing to burn. Like the heads, the bodies remained above, though they did not circle, did not fly, instead they hung static, as though they had been pegged to a line, their fists clenching and unclenching compulsively.

"Perhaps the guillotine will be satisfied now it's had its meal," said Father, but that night, the oldest residents that now remained were to be found leaving their homes and stepping into the sky, eager to offer their necks to the blade.

Unlike the guillotine's night-time only entreaties, the heads had a voice during the day, and their song became the town's constant companion. Although the tone of the singing was sweet, it was not a song that pleased. It made shoulders hunch and skin crawl. Chests tighten and gums bleed.

People began to walk with cotton wool in their ears. To keep their eyes cast down on the ground ahead of them so as not to catch sight of the cleanly cut necks that circled above. They wore raincoats and hats to stop the constant fine drizzle of blood from staining their clothing.

Night after night, the guillotine begged, and the most senior in age that remained complied, adding their heads to the growing blanket of singing skulls that was being knitted. It became clear that the wooden beast planned to clean its plate.

"We should leave town," said Laurie, and her parents agreed, going so far as to pack their cases and put on their coats, but for some reason they remained. For some reason everyone in town remained, despite it all. No one questioned why they stayed, some hypnotic side-effect of the song of the cut heads, perhaps. All that matters is that they did not leave, and the feast continued.

By the end of the third week, the town was cast in a permanent gloom, so many in number were the swirling heads and static bodies that covered the sky. A gruesome lid had been constructed that blocked out the sun. Still, the guillotine kept its regular hours, silent by day, mournfully desperate at night.

Many longed to feed themselves to the guillotine. Impatient for when it would be their turn to joyfully join the ascended. Felt a strange revulsion that they remained below. Remained whole.

"I won't go," said Jackson Porter as he and Laurie walked the shrouded streets, the song of the heads loud and sharp and all-pervasive.

"Me neither," replied Laurie, but she knew he must feel the itch the same as she did. Each night that passed, the oldest people remaining became younger and younger. The line was moving down and down, soon the elders would be teenagers. The pull of the singing heads, of the guillotine's own baleful pleading, tugged at her with increasing ferocity.

"What d'you think it feels like, to be consumed?" she asked.

"Don't care and I'm never going to find out," he replied brusquely.

"Maybe... maybe it feels sort of... good."

Laurie was the last member of her household. Her mother, five years younger than her father, had joined him above two nights previous. Laurie had begged, had tried her best to keep hold of her, to prevent her from stepping up and up towards the blade, towards the joyfully singing heads of her grandparents, of her father. She'd hung on to her with desperation, but her mother had shoved her aside, eyes never leaving the sky, her mouth pulled into a buoyant, eager smile.

"Please don't leave me," Laurie had said, even as the blade did its work and her mother's head rushed to join those of her family.

———

Soon enough, there were no adults left at ground level, all had gone to the guillotine. Jackson Porter, despite his firm protestations that he would do no such thing, had offered himself up to the starving blade the previous night. Laurie had watched as he stepped jubilantly into the sky. Watched as he kneeled beneath the blade and his head was hungrily cleaved from his body.

On her final night, Porter's head lingered outside her bedroom window, singing a personal invitation, an invocation. Laurie opened the shutters her father had installed for protection and watched Porter sing, his eyes wide and fixed upon hers, tears of happiness streaking down dark cheeks as his blood dripped, painting the steps below that lead to her front door. Laurie did not bother to resist. Did not lock the door and toss the key away. Did not attempt to climb into bed to sleep. Instead she bathed, carefully washing each part of herself. She slipped on her finest dress and stepped out onto the street as the guillotine mewled expectantly. Laurie gazed up at the swarm of singing heads and readied herself to re-join her family.

AUTHOR BIO

Matthew Stott is an author and publisher and has written for BBC television and radio. His novels include the middle-grade books *A Monstrous Place*, *The Identical Boy*, and the urban fantasy series *Hexed Detective*. Find him on Twitter: @MattStottWrites

Avalanche

by Briana Morgan

We just left base camp one and my hands are so cold even in their gloves that the ache spreads up my arms.

Evie sighs. I turn my body so she doesn't see me tense.

"You didn't have to come." As if to silence me, the wind presses my mask against my lips. "You *wanted* to. You told me—"

"I know what I said," she snaps.

"It's not like K2. You can turn back. I won't hold it against you."

"Shut up. Jesus."

I'm unsure what's more biting, her tone or the air up here. The latter thins by the minute.

One last climb before I die. One last climb before the cancer...

The wind whips ice against my cheeks. Evie swears.

"Green Boots."

"What?"

"Green Boots. He's our next marker."

I try not to think about our friends farther up the mountain or the chemo and how it makes my stomach burn, how everything I vomit up is stringy spit and acid.

The world shifts underneath us as the earthquake hits. The first wave of snow bowls us over. Cold wetness creeps over the back of my neck, soaks through my clothing. Ice scrapes my wrist. I can't scream or I'll choke.

Avalanche. Every climber's worst fear.

The onslaught of numbing white envelops us. Snow presses against my chest, constricting my lungs.

A crunch breaks the silence, and her hand squeezes my shoulder.

I swear I feel Evie's desperation before she calls my name. When you've been with someone for so long, you can't help feeling everything they feel, too.

I reach through the snowbank and grab her, jerking her toward me. She curls against my chest with my arms wrapped around her.

She gasps. "I shouldn't have said—"

"Evie. We need to save our oxygen."

"Sorry," she says.

I say nothing back. There is only the cold silence and the fate I can't escape.

Death always finds a way.

AUTHOR BIO

Briana Morgan (she/her) is a horror author and playwright. Her books include The Reyes Incident, The Tricker-Treater and Other Stories, Unboxed: A Play, and more. She's a proud member of the Horror Writers Association, the Science Fiction & Fantasy Writers Association, and the Alliance of Independent Authors. When not writing, Briana enjoys gaming, watching scary movies, and reading disturbing books. Briana lives in Atlanta with her partner and two cats.

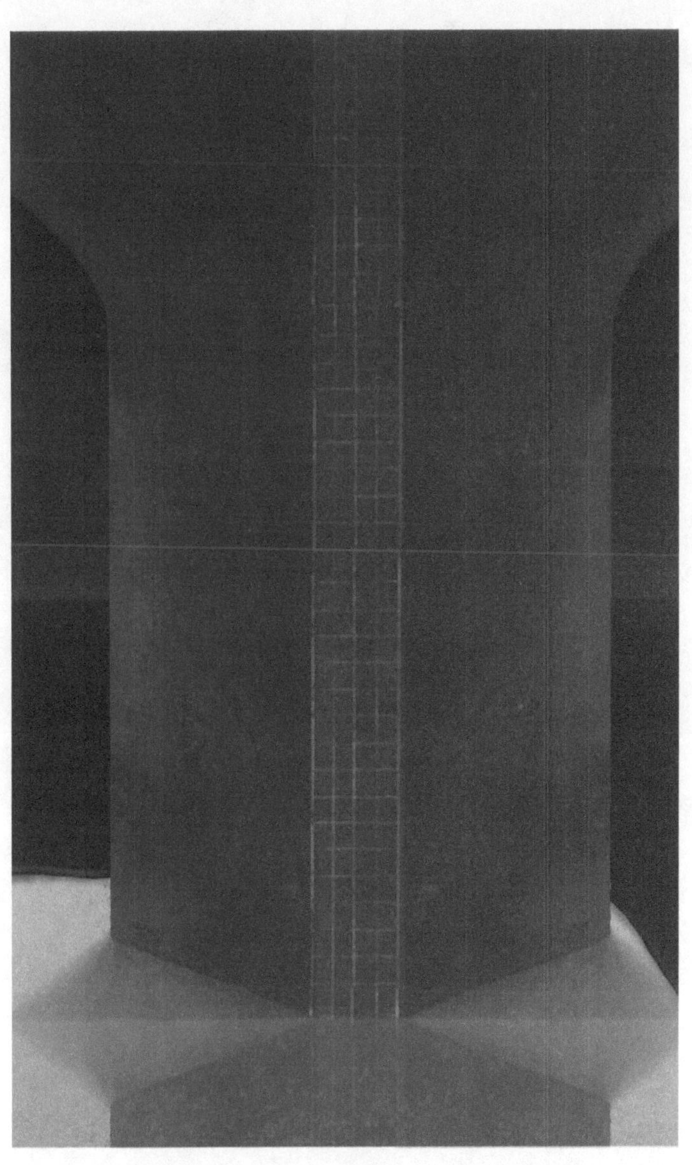

The Cicatrix

by James Bennett

London, now

Yeats once wrote that the world was full of magic things if only we were keen enough to see them. Magic was on Yardley's mind this December morning as his bones creaked from another toilet-interrupted sleep in his cramped Balham flat. Coughing, he staggered into the bathroom at the end of the hall. His mouth was a haunt of rum, cigarettes and the taste of burnt moths. Bearing a hangover worthy of Nero, he stumbled for the khazi, disgorged the remnants of yesterday's supper onto porcelain. His locket, gold-dulled-to-brass, hung open at his neck. It displayed the flash of a young and impudent smile between full brown lips.

He couldn't remember the day it was taken. Seb was thirty years in his grave. Vanished. Like everything was vanished these days.

A shit. A wash. When he rubbed the steam from the mirror above the sink, he reflected that he no longer saw magic things at all, not in the purest sense. All he saw was his seventy-six-year-old face in the glass. Audiences across Europe had once called him 'magisterial', but he could no longer see why. His stern lips and pale skin had all become haggard, a map of a life ill-lived. Of too many cocktails, meaningless sex and a weight of guilt.

Of murder, his conscience croaked, the only voice left to it. The sparks of his eyes were blunted. Soured by bitterness.

No magic things. Strange for a magician to admit. A rejection at the end of things when friends, fame and money had gone. When no lovers remained to lick his shrivelled balls and there was a demon staring at him from the bathroom mirror.

"Sad," said Ormenus, servant of the Scale of Six, the Author of All Calamities. In the glass it looked as blue as the morning, cherubic and levitating. "Ladies and gentlemen, witness the fall of the Great Magus, Yardley Becket Ward. Once the rival of Marzan of Magnificent himself. Now ignorant of his own summoning."

Balls. Yardley shut his eyes. Like a streak of unbidden piss, the memory of last night came flooding back to him. The diagram on the floor of the living room. The grimoire (*De Occulta Philosophia*, Agrippa), open on the floorboards. The candles, the bowl and the dead moths. The sigils in cat's blood. The *khetem* clutched in his fist. And the demon, Ormenus, who'd come at Yardley's bidding moments before he'd blacked out.

"Gah," Yardley spat. "*Exi, seductor.* I've changed my mind. Fuck off back to Hell."

Ormenus, all fangs and swishing tail, chuckled.

"Then you'll need another cat, magus." Salt and gravel was its voice, resounding from beyond the world. "Or do you imagine your words alone hold power? Those heady days are gone."

Yardley growled, his knuckles white on the edge of the sink.

"We all do things we regret."

"That's putting it mildly," Ormenus replied. "Thirty years you've had from me, afforded you by the Province. And a pretty price you paid for them too." The demon jabbed a claw at the locket around the old man's neck. "Isn't that why I'm here? *Seb* was the name on your lips last night."

As if made of putty, the creature in the glass moulded itself to resemble the young man in question. The high, clear brow and strong nose. The dark eyes that had first arrested Yardley in Cairo back in '82. And his smile, dazzling as the Nile. Forever frozen in the picture in the locket.

Seb Hassan Samir. Dead these past three decades. *Dead and burning.*

As if he could forget...

If the old man's face had been wrinkled before, now it looked like a sphincter, threatening to cave in on itself. He snapped the locket shut, a protective, futile gesture; the demon knew his heart. Outside, a car hooted. A train rattled past, the passive-aggressive business of London a million miles away. The pain in his chest climbed up his throat, exploding in a shout that barely echoed in the cramped space. He raised a fist and smashed it against the mirror, the glass crumpling inward.

The demon grinned at him from sixty shards.

Seb. But it began with Marzan. The remembering.

"The black star is back," Ormenus told him. "Will you make your peace with God, magus? Or with me?"

Cambridge and London, 1972

Along with Harry Blackstone Jr. and Marzan the Magnificent, Yardley Becket Ward had been considered one of the greats. At his peak, he was the toast of clubs from Moscow to Madrid. It didn't start out that way though. Not long after graduating, a fair haired, dazzling young man with an equally bright future ahead of him, he'd been seduced from the promise of a literary career by Magic School. Magic, back then, held no hint of the paranormal. As far as he understood it, the work of magicians involved illusions and practiced deception, that was all. And practically minded, Yardley had applied himself. By autumn of his gap year, a stack of books about magic had amounted in his bedroom at home to obscure one half of the window. The birds in the apple tree outside had no idea of the trials they were about to be subjected to.

A talent for vanishing coins and floating cards soon taught him that he could make money at it, first at the parties of friends, later in a small Northampton theatre. While he was treading those dusty boards to modest applause, Evander Marzan (not 'the Magnificent' then) was lighting up the backstreet theatres of London. The young prodigy with his handsome Greek looks, quirky top hat and mysterious smile was on his way to big time.

"He *is* admirable," Yardley had argued with his father, the old man scowling at Marzan's first appearance on breakfast

TV in their ramshackle Fen Ditton cottage, a place left to them after Lily, his mother, passed away from cancer two years before. "It does take a certain skill. As it happens, I've been thinking of moving to London myself. Make a go of it."

"And kiss your life goodbye, idiot. Do you know how much it cost us to send you to Christchurch?"

Yardley, who'd found a new hero, had left his father wheezing and swearing at the box and indeed embarked for the city in question. He rented a flat in Camberwell where the traffic on the roundabout outside shook his window all night and filled his tiny room with fumes. He practised rope tricks. Shuffled cards. Produced doves from handkerchiefs. When he got bored he went to Soho pubs, drank lots and laughed lots. He went home with policeman and dancers, all of them good-looking, all of them forgettable. His heart was set on the stars.

When he read in *The Stage* that Marzan was advertising for an assistant for his upcoming show (*Fantastikós!* the posters screamed from Paddington to Saint Paul's; the magician was gathering steam in the capital), Yardley went along, borne on nerves and the hope in his heart.

"An interesting act of restoration," Marzan told him from where he sat in the auditorium, a silhouette of dark curls and broad shoulders through the footlights. His voice matched his aura, deep and rich. The magician looked ready to burst from his shirt, all Hellenic muscle and verve that didn't help the butterflies in Yardley's belly. "What else can you show me?"

Yardley tried to disappear the red in his cheeks as if that's what Marzan had asked of him. They were in a musty place on Long Acre, adrift in London's theatreland. On the verge of greatness. Yardley knew this was his chance. Gently, he set the book he'd torn in two and then magically healed on the little table beside him. Swallowing, he closed his eyes. Concentrated. Flourished. Fancied he heard a gasp and cracked one eye open to see the book levitating a foot or so next to him.

"Impressive!" Marzan clapped his hands and laughed. Then he dismissed the theatre manager and his agent, and fixed Yardley with a brilliant smile. "What are you doing for lunch?"

Later, after too much wine, Marzan left his top hat propped on the knob of the bed in his hotel room as they fucked, the magician and his prospect. Clinging to the bedstead, grunting into a pillow, Yardley imagined that every thrust of those strong Greek thighs brought him a step closer to success. The old man would be so proud of him! Perhaps he could send some money home, once *Fantastikós!* was up and running, and his name was on everyone's lips in the West End.

Yardley Becket Ward. Assistant. Protégé. *Magician.*

Marzan left for the theatre before dinner, citing further auditions to get through. Standing in a gleaming Leicester Square, Yardley had wanted to joke that there was no point now, surely. Instead, he'd scribbled down his name and address on the back of an old train ticket.

"Promise me...Evander." He dared the name, squeezed the magician's arm. No one was looking. Hell, they could've been brothers for all London knew. "Call me."

His heart was like wax in those fierce eyes. It beat in time with the roar of the traffic and the rain, the particulars of a world from which he was ascending.

Magic, magic things...

As promised, Yardley got a call three days later. He'd barely slept, barely ate, waiting for the telephone to ring. In a crisp monotone, a man who identified himself as Marzan's agent told Yardley that sadly, he hadn't made the cut. The phone cord bit into his hands as he twisted it. Wings of shadow seemed to flutter through the room.

"Truth be told, we're looking for someone younger," the agent told him. "Better luck next time."

London to Luxor, 1972 – 1982

There isn't a joy the world can give like that it takes away, Byron once wrote. A later version of Yardley, successful, adored, had liked to scoff at that. It was a party piece of his. He'd challenge the poets he'd read at Cambridge with a thousand *bon mots* in a thousand bars from London to Luxor, the choicest (and most attractive) of his coterie laughing at every one.

"Why, one can always seek out new joys," he'd say, his Mai Tai swinging in his hand. "Cocaine. The horses. Buggering an avid fan. Byron certainly did."

Then, with a skill as slick as any he'd displayed on stage, he'd make his drink disappear like a rabbit in a hat, and call out for another.

Awareness of one's arrogance, Yardley found, came with age. Years slipped by between his early days in London and eventual fame, a decade filled with shows, nameless lovers, magazine features and fathoms of drink. And magic. *Real* magic. At first, it had only been the odd séance among friends, the petitioning of the dead for favours. The location of a buried chest. The power of fear over a nightly audience. Such amusements had fired Yardley's mind and led him to unmarked bookshops in Glastonbury and York. In a couple of years, he'd read everything from *The Discoverie of Witchcraft* to *The Book of the Law*. A year after that he was practicing ritual from untitled tomes, adding spice to his shows, a spring to his step. He drank rum and smoked cheroots. A little in-cantation never hurt anyone, he'd say. He was a seeker after the truth. The orgies, the bacchanalia came later. The press lapped up his mystique.

Besides, why wouldn't he feel proud of his blood, sweat and tears, the hours he'd put in to prove himself worthy? For a while, the magic had worked like a dream. Pain had seen him scale to new heights. Money had rolled into his bank account. Marzan had his rival.

———

London, now

Humility wasn't a welcome gift. When one could no longer get up the stairs in one go and sex without the aid of Viagra and cash was a faded dream, one tended to soften one's crowing. The years had climbed up his back and twisted it, bending him like a priest's crook (though he'd never been so holy). Time had spun his locks into strands of yarn, raked over his skull. The stride that had carried him out before the footlights of Paris, Berlin and Rome had become a shuffle, accompanied by the applause of his cane.

And the black star, as the demon had told him, was back.

"It was inevitable," he said to the here and now, the cluttered living room of his Balham flat. He regarded the debris of last night's ritual with a twinge in his belly. Around him, books towered with their wealth of knowledge, from *The Key of Solomon* to *De Nigromancia*. The old, stacked relics. A cracked ball of glass. A cup that Judas Iscariot was said to have drunk from. All seemed useless in the face of it. It had all relied on the *khetem*, after all. "The house always wins."

Doctor Sallow had told him as much in his High Road practice last Tuesday, the result of the X-rays spread out on his desk. He hadn't used such flowery speech. The cancer, miraculously in remission since Yardley's forties, was back, a black star over his heart. The tumour, of course, was malignant. *Hungry.* How could he tell the dour, perfunctory man behind the desk that he'd staved off the disease with spells, with an offering made to Hell? With innocent blood, no less. Sallow attempted a commiserating smile, a smile for a septuagenarian patient who refused all advice, still smoked twenty a day and swore far more than was polite. When he gave him six weeks to live (at best), Yardley had nodded. It *was* inevitable. Death was coming for them all. Even bargaining for time had not managed to retain his youth and its pleasures.

At least you know where you're going, he thought.

He shuddered, a chill that the heavy drapes were unable to check. Then he sought out another bottle of rum, half-rolled under the sofa. Instead of clearing up as he'd intended, forgetting the whole infernal idea, he grabbed the packet of Viagra from the escritoire, downed two of the little blue pills and began to relight the candles.

Where was I? He found his spectacles under the armchair, turned his attention to the grimoire. And the *khetem,* snatching the relic from the shelf.

Ah, yes. Seb.

———

Time was the true magician, he knew. It made all things disappear. People, cities, empires... Memory was the great decoy, the wave of a pristine glove on stage, the flutter of doves from a cape. Still, one couldn't stave off the end forever. Shakespeare and his Lady were right. What was done could not be undone. Or so they said.

Yardley hoped to change things, if he could.

"We were in the Scarab Club, Cairo," he told the circle he knelt in, the candlelight and the drawn curtains kind to his naked state. He pouted at his belly with its ladder of silver fuzz, his swelling cock below it. He'd always been a tall man, well hung and rugged. He'd never felt smaller than this. "The summer of '82. I was shit-talking Marzan at the bar, the money-grabbing fraud. That was the first time we met, Seb and I."

"Tell me," Ormenus hissed.

The Author of All Calamities was lying on its back on the ceiling, the flames of its eyes fixed on the renewed ritual. The *remembering.* Yardley had taken up the thread of the spell, a homespun combination of Egyptian sex magick, Enochian channelling and Kabbalistic conjuration. In his mind, the invocation was a bloom of power. Hieroglyphics and Latin wound like thorns around his thoughts, keeping him sharp. The floorboards bit at his knees.

He focused on his avatars, the sigil of the god Atum who'd masturbated the world into existence. The statuette of the Theban god Min, he of the permanently erect phallus. And the sketch of King Camara, ripped from John Dee's *Heptarchia Mystica*, the angel of summoning. Each one was set within the circle. His was a masculine sorcery. In his blood, the drugs flowed.

The demon watched, enthralled. Had Ormenus tracked the withering of his flesh over the last three decades, the breadth of its fiendish bargain? More likely it merely saw a mortal, a soul wavering in the darkness. With every breath, Yardley drew nearer the Gates of Hell, his body growing weaker, betraying the magician as Time betrayed all, no matter their ambition.

"He never laughed at my jokes," Yardley said, his voice thickening along with his cock. In his mind, etched as deeply as the *khetem*, the cylinder seal between his knees, Seb Samir was standing beside him in the crowd. He was a slender figure in a pinstripe suit, his fez atop his impeccable hair like a boat on the Nile at night. Steve Miller was singing *Abracadabra* on the record player, annoyingly. It was the young man's eyes that had stuffed all the witticisms down Yardley's throat and eventually caused his hangers-on to drift away, drunk and in search of more eloquent amusements. "Oh, what a distraction he was. I recall I was quite rude to him at first. I told him I didn't have any money." Seb had smiled and touched his elbow, lightly. "Then he asked for a job."

"Yes, yes. He was your assistant for ten years, before the black star rose. He was helping you into cupboards. Sawing Barbara in half." The demon flapped a claw, impatient. "Get to the good bit."

Yardley choked. Demon or no, he wanted to tell the thing on the ceiling that he hadn't taken Seb to his hotel room that very night. That he hadn't plied the younger man with promises, rum and cocaine. That he'd taken him for a walk instead. Yes, that was a better story, albeit a false one. A pleasant walk past the Al-Azhar Mosque or through the maze of the Khan el-Khalili. How they'd discussed Bolingbroke and Paracelsus as if he'd known them, the two of them almost touching, their hands close, wary of strangers in the Saharan night. It was an image that Yardley had sold himself over the past thirty years, vivid enough to be true, yes. A way to tell himself that he'd been a better man.

Once.

There was no fooling a servant of the Scale of Six. Lies were their oxygen, their daily bread.

"I never thought I'd see him again," Yardley confessed, stroking himself. His balls dangled like bruised plums. Lord, it was hard to stay hard, even with the pills. "His naivety bored me. I simply wanted to show off. Bigging myself up, as it were. I told him how I'd read the poets at Cambridge. How I got into the magic. Parlour tricks first and then...the real stuff. The truth is I was going to fuck him and kick him out of my room." He coughed, throbbing in his hand. "Hell, I'm only human. It was the sex that made me think twice. And the talk of tombs."

"Tell me."

And he did. With mounting jerks and shortening breath, the magician wanked out the memory.

Cairo, 1982

Seb was on his knees within minutes of entering Yardley's hotel room. The young man had barely taken in the ivory-and-gold fittings of the four-poster bed, the gleaming, if tacky, touches that adorned the Marriott Ramses before they'd torn the place down in the 90s. Printed pharaohs stared down from the walls, nameless and kohl-eyed. Outside, palm trees hissed in the night. The noise of traffic on the Nile Corniche wafted into the room with the heat, the sand and the stink of the river. Yardley paid them no mind. He let his new assistant unzip him and pluck out his cock—it'd needed no help to stiffen in those days—and taken him in his mouth, warm between his lips. Seb had taken in the head of him like an overripe plum, his tongue dancing down the underside of his shaft, then returning to swallow him once more. Deeper this time. Harder. The youth's fingers, butter-smooth, formed an oscillating ring. Root to bud. Bud to root. The rhythm matched the gallop of his breath.

A better man would've told the youth it wasn't necessary. The then-thirty-six-year-old magician *did* need help, both off stage and on. He could afford to pay for it too. A better man would've refrained from this interview—no, liberty—in the name of professionalism. It was unlikely that Seb was any different from the other prospecting Cairenes in the city. He was poor, streetwise, keen to escape the confines of his desert-and-camel-shit world, surely. He also knew about magic, *real* magic, but Yardley didn't know that at the time. All he'd known was the spell underway, his fingers tangling in the young man's hair, the fire between his legs. When he'd pulled Seb away, saliva dotting the carpet, his new assistant looked up at him with eyes like burning stones.

"Use me," he'd gasped. "Master. *Sidi.* I am yours."

"Don't talk." Yardley wrenched Seb up by his hair. One hand tweaked his nipple. The other grabbed the bulge in his pants. "That's my first stipulation. Shut the hell up and take off your clothes."

Seb obeyed. Cotton ripped under shaking hands, smooth brown muscle under it. A thick, circumcised cock sprang from his yanked down trousers. Buttocks parted with the firmness of gourds. At that point, Yardley recalled, Seb couldn't have talked if he'd wanted to. Both of them were gasping for air. Particles of sand were in their eyes. Their lungs. Shadows danced.

Talk would come later, through cigarette smoke on silk pillows. The young man told Yardley about the wonders of the desert, the ghosts, the djinn and the demons (and the treasures they guarded) that lingered in buried tombs. The resources waiting to be tapped... On that distant, lustful night, the 'Great Magus' had thought himself the teacher. He'd taken his assistant roughly—as graceless and inept as any lad he'd fucked in the dorms of Corpus Christi—the bedstead banging against the wall while Yardley ploughed the young man to a swift and sweaty culmination.

It was no more than sex back then. The rest would come later, much like a curse.

Along with the black star. His cicatrix.

———

London, now

With a bark, Yardley came on the floorboards. His balls ached, jism splattering the circle. Barren. Already growing cold. Tears dribbled from the corners of his eyes and not merely with the effort.

This is the worst part of the ritual. Behind his ribs, his heart flopped like a fish on land. *Remembering Seb. What I did to him...*

Atum, Min and King Camara looked on without passion. Sweat stung his eyes, blurring the scene. Christ, he needed a cigarette. And rum.

"Are you...satisfied, demon?" The creature above him might as well have sat in the royal box of his memory, watching it play out with relish. Wasn't that why he'd summoned it here, to feast on the meat of his past joys, devouring them in exchange for...what? One last glimpse before the end?

Peace? Yardley would've laughed, had he the breath. "Haven't I shown you enough?"

No magic things...

"You're pathetic," Ormenus told him, like gravel crunching under boots. "Do you think the faded pleasures of a dying old man hold much weight with the Six? Look at you now, Ward. Lower than the belly of a worm."

Candles guttered, strewn by Yardley's outstretched limbs. With the last of his strength, he rolled onto his back and glared up at the Author of All Calamities. The cherub leered down at him with a snakelike tongue. With fat, judgemental eyes.

"Let me see him. *I beg you!*"

His Balham flat dulled his roar. Drama had been stripped from him too, it seemed. Once he'd relied on theatrics so much, distraction, smoke and mirrors. *The good old days...* Time had left him no puff of smoke, no trap door to escape through. The demon saw him for what he was. And yet he still put on this performance.

"It isn't joy I want, magus. It's *pain.* The most painful memory of all."

"Please..."

Ormenus laughed, a scatter of knives. The thing was melting into the plasterwork, a scaly Cheshire Cat. It was called back to the Province for some awful task or other. With a flick of its tail, a sneer, it was gone. But not before Yardley had gauged the depth of its mercy, as shallow as a young man's grave in the darkened room.

Between his knees, he clutched the *khetem*, its intaglio of glyphs impressed on his skin.

In one eye, an unseen spark.

Cairo, 1982

The Saqqara sands have ever swirled with mystery. And memories buried deep.

"'Come ye, blower of knots'," Seb had said that morning in the Ramses Hotel, the morning of their trip to the necropolis. The phrase, Yardley knew, was Ancient Egyptian for 'magician', one who'd worked with cords and bindings to heal (or inflict) pain back in the Old Kingdom. The innuendo was clear, of course, borne out by the wink his assistant gave him. The young man was growing cheekier by the day. One too many fucks had assured him of the 'Magus's' lust, if nothing else.

What else is there? Lord knew Yardley had made no promises. As he climbed into the jeep that would take them down the Western Agricultural Road and into the Governate, scarves over their noses and mouths, he made a mental note to slap Seb down at the earliest opportunity. Physically, if necessary. The *shabab* was getting ideas above his station.

Who does he think he is? He scowled at Seb's grin. Something in his chest ached at the question, and he wondered, and was afraid. *Does he think I'm in love?*

It was only later, in the quarried heart of Saqqara, a labyrinth of excavated pits, crumbling valleys and wind-gnawed pyramids that Yardley lit again on the question. In the meantime, awe gripped him. All around, the strewn rubble of Memphis stretched out under the sun, the sunken mastabas and the catacombs of the eastern cliff, all dedicated to the goddess Bastet. The palms along the Nile were an army of bones, seething in the dust. The site was famous for its numerous tombs, its gilded coffins and godly idols. The unearthed caches of mummies—not only human, but animal too, cats, cobras, lions, and even scarab beetles. All eviscerated and pickled for the afterlife (a recollection that the here-and-now Yardley in his flat, steeped in rum, couldn't help but see as ironic).

On that day, he'd been cynical and forty years younger. Most finds at Saqqara, their guide Asim informed them as they climbed the rocky slope, had since been sequestered in the Museum of Antiquities, their mystery locked behind glass. But not all. There were tombs, he said, known only to the wise. Some plundered, yes, and plundered again over the years. And some tombs where no robber would go, deterred by the curses carved on their doors, the threat of a hundred violent deaths down the generations.

Yardley, with an amateur's conceit, was keen to put his own spells to the test. In the details of one scroll, purchased from a one-armed man in the Khan el-Khalili, Seb had assured him they'd found the key. By the time Asim led them over the rise and down a shallow trench (where, their guide went on, the archaeologists had stopped digging in the 70s), Yardley was swatting at flies as much as he was his own nerves. His Ralph Lauren shirt was damp, his teeth on edge. He stood here at last on the brink of greatness. He could feel it, his heart fat with anticipation. A Pharoah's mask. A chest of jewels... The magician was going to be rich, rich beyond his wildest dreams. He'd be the talk from New York to Nanking. Folks would speak of him in the same breath as Evander Marzan, the so-called 'Magnificent'.

Instead, they found a hole in the ground. The stone rolled back, the curse (he'd thought) dispelled by his chant. Yardley had regarded Seb's chagrin under the beam of his flashlight, the hieroglyphics on the wall beyond fluttering along with their shadows. There was no gold. No jewels. No *dead.* Only chambers filled with dust. Caskets long rotten. In the gloom, Seb couldn't see how his fist shook, anchored at his side. Yardley might've struck him then. It might've been the first time (Asim hadn't dared come within fifty feet of the tomb and wouldn't have heard them anyway) if not for the object in his assistant's hand.

"Look, *sidi.* Look what I found."

With a scowl, Yardley had taken in the item the young man held. Along its length, he made out figures in bone—ivory, he thought—the faint wink of gold at either end. Anger melted again into greed. His fingers uncurled, reaching for the thing. The wand or the—

"It's a *khetem.* A cylinder seal," his assistant told him. "A relic from the Old Kingdom."

"Only this?" Yardley asked. His eyes, resentful, darted around the tomb. Blank walls faced him and he tried to keep the pique from his voice. "Is it worth anything?"

Seb nodded. "A few thousand at a guess. But," he held up a hand at Yardley's snarl. "A relic like this holds more value than Egyptian pounds, master."

A long sigh, dry as the air. "This better be good."

"According to *The Book of the Dead,* a relic like this was used to summon and bind demons..."

At this point, the memory grew fuzzy, curdled as it was with wishful thinking, lovemaking that likely never was. Decades later in his cramped Balham flat, a spent Yardley Becket Ward, the onetime Great Magus, clung to it anyway, to the lingering pulse in his flaccid cock. At the time, hadn't he given a bark of joy, pushed the young man up against the wall of the tomb? Surely he had, pressing Seb's face to Anubis, Osiris and Set, the blind, dead gods of the past. Why, he distinctly recalled his sacrilege, unbuckling Seb's belt and yanking his pants down. Yardley had dropped to his knees along with them. His assistant had gasped as Yardley's stubble rubbed against him, his dusty hands forcing his buttocks apart. Grunting, he'd drank in his *shabab—his—*sweat, musk and the faint smell of shit, his tongue seeking out the softest part of him.

Does he think I'm in love? Do I...?

The image rippled, a mirage. Sand came whispering through the cracks in the wall, pouring like blood into the tomb. Every grain bore a weight of guilt, collected over decades. Dreams lost and hopes faded. *Seb. My Seb...* The chamber was filling up with the stuff, a rising tide, the gulp of the desert swallowing them whole. In the lie of his mind, Seb screamed as the sands flooded his mouth, his throat, his glittering eyes. Into the darkness, the two of them spun, sucked into the Saharan womb along with empires, tombs and the memory, the riddles of Time both real and imagined.

What did it matter now?

London, now

On his knees in his flat, naked, cold, Yardley clutched the *khetem.*

Hell wasn't through with him yet.

"That wasn't the day, was it?" Ormenus said. Yardley wished it wouldn't do that with its eyes, the shadows under them like ink. It was edging the circle, its horns a foot above the tallest candle. "The day he died."

"Nor was it the first time I hit him." *Or the last.* The magician was cross-legged, drunk on the living room floor. It was night and he was making his second attempt at the bargain, the *khetem* placed under his arse. Best not let the Author of All Calamities see the relic, lest it suspect a ruse. Sodium from the street outside leaked in through the curtains, the orange pall of London. Shadows draped the books and the knick-knacks in the room, the tomes and the souvenirs from his travels. A Hand of Glory he'd found in Normandy. A scrying glass from Prague. *Gris-gris* from Louisiana. None were suited to this particular task. "That was in Israel much later. The first time..." He coughed, a hitch in his throat. Why was it still so difficult to say? "The first time he cheated on me. Some businessman from Saudi. Said he was a prince." He gave a laugh, sharp as water in a frying pan. *Not the last time for that either.* "Oh, Seb didn't know about my glass. Or how I watched him on occasion. I saw the whole thing, you know."

"And it made you hard."

"I'm a man, demon."

"That isn't what I meant," Ormenus said. "This is all quite juicy, I'm sure. But these memories are like bruises around the wound. The hole in you. The black star. Let me get my tongue in there, magician. Let me lick up the pain, the way you licked—"

"All right. All right. I'm getting there."

"No. You're stalling."

Indeed, you fucker. Behind my eyes, and around my skull, I'm reciting a charm. But you don't need to know that...

"It hurts to open up a scar, demon," Yardley said.

Aperi ostium inferni.

Wasn't it obvious? It's why Ormenus had come. Why a servant of the Scale of Six had been diverted from a thousand daily mortal petitions, drawn from the heaps of slaughtered pets, spilled spunk and burning insects to attend to an old and washed up magician. Like all temptations, some memories were fish and chips. Some were *foie gras.* The summoning called to the demon and the demon must heed. But it wasn't obliged to give him what he wanted...

"You had your time in the sun," Ormenus replied, fingernails on the inside of a coffin. "From Egypt to Rome to the shrine of Parnitha. And *beyond.* By the turn of the millennium, you'd surpassed Marzan himself."

Evander, you cunt. Mention of the Greek magician, tawny and svelte in a way that Yardley had never been, was a knife through his heart. Marzan had always worn that stupid hat as if to convey the idea that he was taller, better than anyone else in the Circle. *You might be food for the worms, but you owe me. I paid such a high price...*

The demon, of course, was loving it. "Truth be told, the black star was a gift. But you were headed for the Province regardless, whether you'd died thirty years ago or not." The demon grinned at him, swinging its tail. "This is late in the day to try to... alter our agreement."

"I'm still on this side of the gate."

"Not for long, Ward. Not for long. So let's get down to business."

Rome, 1992

The business, as it happened, was death. 'The Carriage held but just ourselves', as Dickinson once wrote. In this case, it had been Yardley and the Reaper in the carriage, rattling over the ruts of a debauched life to the flaming gates of Hell. In Rome, the autumn of '92, he'd collapsed on stage, passing out in a mess of paper flowers and a silver hoop, some tawdry conjurer's trick. Before oblivion claimed him, he'd noted no change in the audience's gasp; this was entertainment of a different kind, but entertainment nonetheless. The light at the end of the tunnel was a spotlight in his frozen gaze, red-tinged and flickering. Hot.

Barbara was still in her leotard, her makeup smeared, when she got him to the hospital. They hooked him up to a drip and an EKG machine. She'd only ridden in the ambulance out of form, he believed, some remote, tenuous sense of duty. On two occasions, the knives during the throwing act had struck her. Once, he'd nicked her thigh with a saw, the consequence of too much rum in his dressing room, for which he reckoned she still held a grudge. The girl looked quite the slattern once the defibrillator plucked Yardley from the carriage and back into the emergency room. She'd likely been crying over the prospect of a missed paycheck. He managed to sit up, but Barbara didn't stay for long. In fact, she never came back. Not merely to the hospital. Ever.

Poof!

Where was Seb, he wondered? The drugs in his veins were drowning him, sucking him into the pillows with all the inexorable weight of Saharan sand. Perhaps his *shabab* had stayed at the theatre, tried to deal with the fallout, the complaints...but his collapse had happened yesterday. If Seb were here, he'd talk to him, he told himself. Ten years had passed since the Scarab Club in Cairo. Perhaps it was high time. He'd tell Seb that he... cared for him, insist that he was still his *sidi. A magic thing.* To prove it, he'd clutch the younger man's hand, bring it to his crotch under the sheets—it was incredible how *horny* a near-death experience could make you—and let them ride out the misunderstanding to a reconciliatory climax. It was the closest he'd ever come to an apology.

The next day, a turnip of a man called Doctor Capello had sat like a restless psychopomp next to his bed and showed Yardley the X-rays. It was his first sight of the black star, the shadow over his heart. Capello had turned the sheets of film over like Tarot cards. Or some ill-starred astrological chart, Death and Pluto-Ascendent.

"Cardiac sarcoma," the doctor told him in English. "You've been overdoing things, *signor.* This European tour of yours..." Capello flapped a hand at the grimy square of glass that passed for a window, dismissing the fully booked venues, the press and the money in a way that vexed him. "You're forty-six years old, Mr Ward. Perhaps it's time to quit the smoking and the drinking, yes? There were traces of amphetamines in your blood. I'm sure you could afford treatment."

Drugged or no, the magician had something to say about that. There were people relying on him, he said. He had appearances to fulfil. He couldn't simply perform 'Becket Ward's Great Vanishing Act' and fuck off into some clinic or other. Didn't the doctor know who he was? *Arcana Europa* was the talk of the continent. He'd been on the front page of *La Repubblica!*

The memory of that day had become as hazy as all the rest, or so it seemed to the older Yardley, drunk on rum in the fiendish future. The truth was he'd said all these things, but nowhere near as politely. Capello had left the magician to his profanity, his tray flung against the wall, and retreated into the gloom of the hospital. Next time, he'd sent a nurse.

For three days, Yardley sat in his hospital bed, his heart burning with more than the cancer. His veins ran thick with sedatives and guilt. Oh, he had ample time to think on his mistakes, all the things he should've done. An elderly father he should've called. Employees he'd never paid. Promises broken and all the pretty lies. Small animals he'd slaughtered. Those he'd cursed.

And a young Egyptian with burning eyes who he'd struck one too many times. Who he'd never told—

Oh, Seb.

Like the tomb at Saqqara, the room threatened to crush him, squeeze out the juice of him onto the floor, acid on linoleum. On the wall hung a picture of the Pope. He smiled down like the avatar of smugness.

For three days, Yardley Becket Ward, the 'Great Magus', sat in his own piss and shit, considered his imminent demise, and wondered where the fuck Seb had gotten to.

———

London, now

"Oh, this is cruel, demon."

"Why, thank you," Ormenus said. He was genuinely flattered, affecting a bow through the candlelight. "Pity is sweet. But this isn't the half of it."

Yardley gagged. Partly it was the near-empty bottle in his hand. Partly it was the moths, crisping in the bowl. The scent was supposed to aid concentration. It couldn't compete with the damp of his flat.

"What Hell..." around his neck, the locket swung, a sad pendulum, "could be worse than this?"

Ormenus chuckled. "Oh, just you wait."

Rome, 1992

Yardley checked out of the Gemelli Hospital the second he could stand, a stooped, coughing Icarus on Francesca Vito waiting for a cab. Doctor Capello had insisted he remain for further check-ups with all the polite insistence of a man who doesn't want guests to stay for dinner. The magician had turned his tumour-bared skull upon him and blown smoke in his face.

No, grazie.

Death was in him, a living part. But the black star was not without power. He'd make sure to use it in the weeks left to him. *Yes!* There was no reason for restraint left, he thought, waving the doctor goodbye, the butt of his fag bouncing off the tarmac. A snatched infant, say, on the right altar, at the right time, could gain him greater influence, a special place in Hell. What fear of the consequences now?

First, he had to find Seb.

There were journalists outside the Palazzo, where his agent had booked him a suite. How they pecked like crows in the rain! Cameras flashed. Onlookers gawped. He was perfectly aware that the sordid details of his private life were often smeared across the press these days, titillation for the gibbering masses. Once, he'd been a gangling youth in London looking at the stars. Now what he'd dreamed of sickened him. In all likelihood, the news of his collapse had been greeted by religious types as proof of his wickedness, the reward for his dabbling in the Black Arts. Further irony, in hindsight, considering he had yet to make use of the *khetem* or attempt anything *truly* demonic. In a funny way, the days following his diagnosis were his last days of innocence.

"No comment," he snapped at the hacks outside the hotel. "Give it a rest, will you?"

He muttered a curse under his breath, wishing all of them a sudden end. His carriage was heading for the Province. There was plenty of room aboard.

In the sanctum of the lobby, he met his agent, Bob Culpepper, who'd flown in from London on wings of anxiety that were shrivelling to fury the longer the magician prevaricated, sequestered in his suite. For days, Yardley refused to speak to the press. He rejected every statement written on his behalf. There was the business of a porter who claimed that the magician had harassed him—nothing a cheque couldn't fix. Venues kept calling. Culpepper fumed. So did investors. Ticket holders wanted their money back. The show must go on.

"If you don't fix this," Culpepper hissed at him one morning over breakfast, "then Marzan will. He's in the city, don't you know? I'm sure a call to his manager could secure an appropriate stand-in."

Culpepper was red-eyed and balding—more so of late, his head resembling Yardley's boiled egg. His words were anything but kind.

"Nice to see you too, Bob." Yardley smirked at the man, raising his tumbler of rum. "Thanks for the flowers you sent to the hospital."

Culpepper had sent no flowers, no more than he'd enquired after his client's health.

Yardley banished the man from his rooms. The next day, he fired Culpepper and called off the tour. *Arcana Europa* was over. What did he care for the yelling outside his door? His agent might give himself a coronary. By that time, robed in silk and soothed by opiates, the magician's attention was on the scrying glass he'd brought along in his suitcase. A disembowelled cat lay in the kitchen of his suite, blood pooling on the marble bar. Dark wings were folding around him. He had no time to spare.

His *shabab,* his lover, was missing.

———

London, now

"I found him in Greece." He was coming to it now, the crux of his undoing. The error he'd made. "He ran off with that bastard. Can you believe it? After everything..."

For a moment, Yardley was a boy again, a hand raised to squint through the footlights. A handsome man smiled at him in the audience. *What else can you show me?* He remembered how Marzan's agent had called him three days later, the sting of the phone cord in his hand. As if the man's words had been a prophecy, age crawled over him like a shell. He shivered on the living room floor.

"He gave you up for dead," Ormenus said. It was amusing to him, to watch these mortals and their fuck-ups.

Grizzled, his hair like string in his face, Yardley gripped the locket around his neck. He'd had it made in Copenhagen years ago, not long after his *shabab's* death. A *memento mori* of sorts. Or an albatross. His other hand fell to the floorboards, the bottle rolling away from him. It seemed as keen to escape him as anything, anyone. He was drunk...but not that drunk. In his mind, symbols danced, invisible and bright.

With the tip of one finger, he stroked the *khetem.*

It seemed so strange to say it, amid this feast of memories.

"He forgot me."

———

Athens, 1992

A spell to drain power. The raising of a ghoul. A word of death. These were on Yardley's mind as he went through customs at Ellinikon International Airport. The caution he'd applied throughout his career, avoiding outright diabolism and certain tomes, had fled the second he'd spied Seb in the glass. Since then, he'd been up to his eyes in the *Codex Gigas*, *The Heptameron* and *The Book of Abaddon*. There were few effective conjurations to extend life. All of them involved consorting with demons, the minions and ambassadors of Hell, the Black Province. Thus he'd embarked on a new education. Marzan, the so-called 'Magnificent', had stolen something from him. Something precious. He didn't know how or why. He could guess.

Evander...

The magician wanted to hurt him, kick him when he was down. Perhaps he'd cast a spell of his own. It was fair to say that Seb was at his peak. His apprenticeship had made him lean, from pulling ropes, carrying props and wrestling with crates. Those boyish looks had surrendered to a strong jaw, thick shoulders and a lithe gait. A flood of curls kissed the collar of his shirt—and so Yardley thought with envy—few could withstand the lure of his eyes. When he recalled Seb's body, his engorged, beautiful cock, screws tightened in his chest. To think of other hands upon them, especially— *God!* By all accounts, Marzan was no stranger to bathhouses, the preening, bearded wolf. When Yardley pictured his ridiculous hat and the teeth that gleamed from posters in Warsaw and Amsterdam, his nails bit into the palms of his hands. Huddled in the back of a cab, a grim-faced rake in a herringbone overcoat, whisking down Piraeus Street for the Aite Theatre, he couldn't imagine Seb's abduction as anything but sorcerous.

"Can't you hurry up? The curtain falls at ten p.m."

The December rain lashed the windows. The windscreen wipers and the driver's curses were better than the crap on the radio, some squealing girl band or other. The Athenian night swept past, a blur of neon and honking traffic. The odd museum or statue flashed by. Above all, the Acropolis blazed, golden in the darkness, the realm of tourists these days instead of supplicants.

I'll squeeze out whatever magic remains...

In his lungs, the cancer burned, smouldering under his pills. The black star throbbed, feasting on his heart. *Christ, I'd kill for a cigarette.* He hadn't packed more than a small case: a change of clothes, a grimoire, the *khetem*, some chloroform and a pistol—and he didn't—intend to stay long in the city. If he couldn't release Seb from the spell that bound him, spiriting him away to this land of ruins and gods, then he'd be gone in a day or two at most...

Thanks to his glass, Yardley had gleaned enough of Seb's schedule to judge where he'd be after the finale. He'd always been a dutiful lad. Loyal... *Ha!* Disgorged from the cab, the driver sped off with further expletives. The magician leant on his cane (the silver skull atop it no consolation for its necessity) and wheezed through the puddles for the stage door. Rain belched from gutters. The fire escape above was a cascade. Shadows and neon winked in the reflections. A black car, a Mercedes, crouched at the end of the alley. The lights out. The driver seat empty. *Good.* The place wasn't much for a reunion, if he could call it that. It was private enough. That's why his *shabab* had parked here.

When Seb emerged from the stage door to check that the alleyway was empty, he didn't notice his former employer at first. His head swung this way and that, making sure that the weather had seen off the press and the worst of the fans, the same way he'd once done for Yardley. Seconds passed. Then he tensed, frozen. He twisted towards the gloom by the trash cans. The car keys he held splashed into a puddle, the echoes an accompaniment to Yardley's greeting.

"Why, Seb?" It was all he asked, shaking his head. "Just tell me why."

Seb took a step backward. He knew the power of the man before him, sick or no. He wasn't about to put it to the test. In his eyes, Yardley could see that Seb knew exactly what he'd done, could gauge the pain he'd caused. There was space left for a hundred things, a hundred excuses his *shabab* could've given him, from sorcery to blackmail. In his long and wounded gaze, Yardley only read intent. A longing for freedom, perhaps. And something else. Something so ugly and horrid it threatened to detonate the star in his chest, a black supernova.

"*Sidi.* Ward. I—"

"You were seeing him before, weren't you?" Every breath was a dropped stone as the understanding came to him. Yardley had to lean on his cane. "For how long? Tell me, do you...?"

Mercifully, his question went unanswered. That was when the stage door opened again. Out came Marzan the Magnificent, his top hat tipped to the rain. He almost walked into his assistant, Seb like ice in the alley, then corrected himself with a grunt. His beard, trim and slick, parted in a rebuke. Time held the space in its grip, the neon a smear of purple and green. The downpour ticked like a clock. Marzan sensed Yardley in the shadows or he followed Seb's gaze. Either way, he turned to the sight of his rival raising a pistol, one black-gloved finger on the trigger.

Spells. Necromancy. Death. In the end, Yardley simply shot the man, the alleyway resounding with the noise. A car backfiring. A crack of thunder. A door slamming shut on betrayal.

Marzan's hat flew off and landed in a puddle. Red joined the reflections.

("Oh, sweet, delicious torment," Ormenus said, floating off the floor and erect, a thousand years away in London. The old man had come to it at last.)

————

Yardley had Seb drive. One didn't argue with a man in the back seat who happened to hold a pistol. Twice, his former assistant—his former *lover*—tried to reason with him. Twice, Yardley hushed him. What the hell could Seb say? Infidelities he'd learned to overlook. He had done so several times as long as they were meaningless. On that night, he was beyond talk, consumed, a spindle of quiet rage in the Mercedes. He watched the sodium glow of Athens give way to the foothills as the car sped north.

Oh, in him was a storm, fierce as any simoom. Every particle a memory trying to pierce his conscience. Seb in the Scarab Club, a hand on his elbow. The sound of his gasps in a forgotten tomb. Nights where the two of them had sprawled, as coupled as crook and flail under the sheets in this or that hotel. Vengeance was shelter too. Pain a wall. With the same degree of concentration he used for his rituals, he distanced himself from the younger man. He was merely a tool now. Bait. Seb would pay for his treachery, yes. The magician had found the method in his book. The *khetem* was the key.

This is all your doing. Your fault.

Trembling, Yardley had Seb pull up as close as possible to the cave on the mountain road. It was near midnight. Mount Parnitha loomed above them, capped with snow under the stars. The Tatoi Forest whispered on all sides, a restless horde in the darkness. The smell of pines spoke of a freshness he would never know again. When Seb killed the headlights, it seemed he sensed his fate in the settling gloom. He turned his tear-streaked face to his captor in one last entreaty.

"*Sidi*, forgive me." His voice was raw, his accent softened by years on the road. His muscles were bunching like a caged tiger. It was clear he would fight, given the chance. "Please. Don't do this. I never loved—"

Liar!

"You're begging the dead." Yardley's eyes were burning too, damn it. He couldn't afford to lose focus, not now. "I'll have one last kindness from you."

Seb gave a sob, turning in the seat. Was there a remnant there, some ghost of affection? Or was he merely crying for himself? It didn't matter now. Finding nothing to help him in the pitch black road, he hung his head, sniffling. Ignoring the pain in his lungs, Yardley pushed himself forward, tugging the chloroform-soaked rag from his pocket—*hey presto!*—and slapping it over his *shabab's* face.

There was a struggle. Then silence.

In the daylight hours, tourists knew the cave on the western flank of Parnitha as the Cave of Pan. In fact (and verified by hours of research), Yardley was certain it had once served as a shrine to Hecate, the goddess of the witches. In books one couldn't find in a library, he'd read how the ancients made sacrifices in the cave, chickens, goats and otherwise, summoning the goddess with blood, beseeching her for favours. A place of power was vital for such an invocation, even if the varying divinities were not. Yardley had learnt as much. Gods were masks of mortal design, nothing more, placed over the sentient chaos of the cosmos to lend it shape and meaning. Since the dawn of time, the entity known as Hecate had danced behind a thousand faces. As had Pan, with his horns and cloven hooves...

The magician had his own preferences. This in mind, he lit the candles around the slab at the rear of the cave. He painted the symbols from his flask of cat's blood. Then he shed his clothes. Seb, drugged and sleeping, he stripped too, a sign of humility. Oblation. As Yardley worked, he numbed himself to the task. His scowl squeezed the moisture from his eyes, the body on the rock a blur. Seb's cock, a lump of flesh devoid of sentiment. His eyes were closed, their magic lost.

There'll be other lovers, he told himself. *A future filled with them.*

His faithless apprentice would secure them for him, another three decades of life. His offering on the stone was the crux of his bargain, tearing the black star from its zenith.

"Oh, Ormenus, the Author of All Calamities, servant of the Scale of Six." Yardley's voice bounced around the cave, the knife shaking in his fist. Under his knees lay the *khetem*, fuelling his invitation. "I summon thee hence. *Venit, seductor.* Accept my sacrifice..."

He gave himself no time to hesitate, to hold the blade from its purpose. Uttering a word of binding, he plunged his fist downward and skewered his *shabab* heart to stone. Blood danced in the candlelight, painting the cavern walls.

There was smoke then, and laughter.

Through it, Yardley looked up to see blue and scaly flesh.

———

London, now

"'How utterly is flown every ray of light'." Yardley, naked and drunk on the floor of his flat, hung his head. The ritual was complete, his seed and the memory proffered, a potent, bitter feast. "Brontë wrote that. How right she was. Your gift was no gift at all."

"Come now," Ormenus said, looking down from where it sat on the bookshelf, replete with the magician's anguish. "A score and ten. That was our bargain. And it's fair to say you made the most of them, magus. You saw your name in lights at Madison Square Garden. Drank an ocean of rum. Fucked from Toronto to Timbuktu. If it hadn't had all caught up with you, who knows what you'd have achieved? A lasting legacy, perhaps."

Yardley was a fool if he'd expected sympathy. The Province didn't know the meaning of the word. Over the years he'd wrangled from Hell, as the footlights faded, the crowds dried up and age closed its claws around him, his suspicions had come to fruition. Regret was a poison. Memory a curse. He could pay others to bury bodies. Invoke spells to cover his tracks. Persuade weaker minds of his presence, his continued isolation in Rome. *Why, detective, I was here all the time. My agent Mr. Culpepper will testify to the fact...* He could mention divine intervention, angels and luck, whenever he regarded the astonishment of doctors, his cancer shrivelling to nothing, the black star dispelled. He could stand at Marzan's graveside (they'd placed his top hat on the coffin), closing his eyes at the sound of dirt on wood and hiding his smile behind his scarf. He couldn't change universal law. That was the cruellest lesson of all. Yes, Shakespeare was right. What was done could not be undone.

Or so they said.

At his side, his fingers closed around the *khetem*. Hieroglyphics pressed into his liver-spotted skin.

"I loved him, you know," he said. It was true that Seb had been with him every night since, a shadow in the wings. In the corner of every hotel room as the magician lay in the shivering foetus of this or that hangover. With this or that whore, none of them a fraction of what he'd lost. "In the end."

What did a demon care about love? Mortal passions held appeal as sustenance alone. Or rather the pain left by their absence.

The Author of All Calamities nodded. "We would not have answered you otherwise."

"And so? Have you considered my plea?"

"Indeed." Ormenus grinned. How it enjoyed dragging out the moment. "Very well. What will it change? I'll grant you your window, magus. Make your apologies brief."

A swish of its tail. A crooked claw. Then the candles were blurring. Heart pounding, Yardley watched the floorboards grow vaporous. The circle of chalk rotated in a way that surpassed his drunkenness. The gloom thickened, the book-shelves, the curtains and the wall eclipsed by a deeper dark-ness. The room shook. His scrying glass shattered on the floor. His avatars, Atum and Min, sank into the portal before him as though into Saharan sand. King Camara, torn from a book, fluttered and danced up by the lampshade, borne on a scorching updraft.

Yes. The cramped confines of Yardley's flat were giving way to a deeper space. A greater kingdom. With a shudder of triumph, Yardley crawled to the lip of Hell.

At last.

His hair, scant as it was, was flailing and crisping in the heat. It didn't bother him. The circle protected him. Clutching the *khetem* to his breast, Yardley Becket Ward, the onetime 'Magus', breathed in the ash and looked down.

If he'd expected fire and brimstone, then he was disap-pointed. No classical Hell for him, it seemed. No fields of lava and blasted rock. No sinners suspended forever in flames. Instead, like a dubious god, he looked down upon a ruined town on a vast cracked plain. Through the miasma, the town seemed at once ancient and modern, a stain on the black sa-vannah. Here, he made out columns, Romanesque and crum-bling. There, the sagging awning of a theatre. A half-buried pyramid. A burnt-out car. The riddle of streets looked like a bullet hole on an emptiness that swirled with twisters of ash. He heard a great wailing on the wind.

In the back of his mind, where glyphs and forgotten di-alects spun—the spell *within* the spell—he wondered what it meant. The town. The land. The lamentation. He'd read that people envisioned the Hell that awaited them, reflecting their own transgressions and crimes, that the damned each held a unique perception. A second later and he was shuddering at the detritus of his own past. Ruins from Rome and Egypt. The stark shell of a Mercedes... It struck him as appropriate that every inferno would be different. Was the wasteland the mirror of his own soul? In the distance, he saw a palace, many turreted and windowless, that he fancied never changed. His heart shrank to see it and he looked away, back to the shattered streets below. Even his eyes refused to travel there.

This is nowhere, he realised. *A void of loneliness. The end of all ambition and lust.*

But not of memory. He winced to think of it, of endless wanderings, parched and alone. Dogged by his sins, which might take an eternity to count. And count again and again, as the undying part of him drifted through the waste. Was this where he'd sent Seb all those years ago? Or was his *shabab* consigned to some deeper realm, a circle of his own making. One of infidelity and treason?

As if culled from ash by the thought, the magician saw the man in question through the miasma. Seb was staggering down the street. *Or what remains of him.* Yes. *What he remembers of himself...* The young man was naked, his once-athletic physique devoured, clothed by the restless waste. His hair, like night, matched the rest of him now. Seb Samir was no more than skin and bone. A ghost, abandoned to a place where time no longer held any meaning. Where the skies howled. The dust danced.

"Seb!"

That was the best that Yardley could muster, a croak swallowed by the wind. Now he was here, prostrate on the threshold, all the words he'd rehearsed in the bathroom mirror, all his apologies dried up in his throat. In his chest, the black star swelled, baleful, threatening to engulf all. The locket swung around his neck, an albatross he'd lose if he could. He wiped his brow, his spectacles dislodged and falling, spinning away in the storm.

Still, Seb looked up.

Sidi.

It was in his mind rather than on the air, Yardley sensed. The ghost below recognised him. Knew him. No joy lit the haunt of his face.

"Make it quick, magus," Ormenus said, speaking from between the boundary of worlds. "I have other fools to attend."

Yardley ignored it. *The fucker.* Bones aching, he was reaching through the hole in the floor. He reached into the Province for Seb, the same way he'd been reaching for him since that morning in Athens when the sun had peeped into his hotel room and told him he'd never again feel its warmth. His heart ached to see that Seb was reaching for him too, spurred by memory. Some faded—

"Stop that," the Author of All Calamities hissed. On their side of the gate, the demon shifted on the bookshelf. Loose pages took to the air, charring above the gulf. "I granted you a moment to speak. No more."

Yardley closed his eyes. The moment his fingers closed on Seb's, the living to the dead, a bolt went through him. Drawing on the last of his strength, he struggled to his knees. In his skull, the wisdom of the ancients flipped over and over, guiding his conjuration. A word of power burst from his lips. He thrust out the *khetem,* the cylinder seal shaking in his fist. Seb's hand was in his now. He was dragging his *shabab,* inch by howling inch, from the clutches of Hell.

One last magic thing...

He knew its name. What he'd promised himself. With a roar, Yardley flung the spell against the bookshelf. The walls shook, his Balham flat quivering with the impact. The relic, recovered years ago from Saqqara, throbbed in his hand. This was its function, no less, the summoning and binding of demons. Ormenus was one such, charged with the business of the Province...and as such, a servant itself.

Who am I if not a master? Yardley had graced the stages of Europe, drunk on ambition and plebian awe. He'd bent the world to his will and grabbed the nape of the future. *Why should now be any different?*

The little blue bastard might mock him. There was no contesting the magician's power. Nursed in his mind for hours, buried under rum and regret, Yardley unleashed the thrust of his spell.

It was to be his greatest trick.

He tightened his grip, fastening on the thing of ash and memory below, the ghost of Seb Samir. With their reunion came memory, the wasteland below rippling and seething with the shapes of the past. A cavern was stretching over his head, symbols daubed on the walls, a bloodstained slab before him. Through a night of rain and regret, a black car hissed in reverse through the mountains, down into the glittering web of Athens. In a shimmering alley behind a theatre, a bullet burst into the muzzle of a pistol. A top hat leapt from a puddle to a handsome Greek head...

Ormenus screamed. The magician barely heard him. Ichor splashed the bookshelf, washing over Paracelsus and Fludd. On one side of the portal, Yardley knelt, the floor shuddering, the demon struggling against the force of the *khetem.* On the other dangled Seb, the filth pouring from him, his smooth brown flesh emerging from the mess. His eyes fixed on the magician.

Yardley?

Yardley gritted his teeth. In his skull rang the spell and the voice of memory. They were reeling, adrift, him and his *shabab,* cast like stones across the surface of Time. On a stage in Rome, the magician leapt from the boards and into the spotlight, his blackout undone. A hundred shows, a thousand applauses, a million faces in the auditorium, all went blurring past like cards spilled from a deck. The Sahara spiralled and churned, burying tombs and secrets. Burying Saqqara. With a thump of impacting sand, the desert took back the *khetem* into its heart.

"Desist! You don't know what you're doing."

The demon could've spoken from anywhere. Behind his eyes, Yardley was back in his hotel room in the Ramses Marriot, lying with Seb on Egyptian silk. Breathless, he dashed away a tear...and found himself looking up at the young man beside him. The past and the future crashed like waves, colliding. It took a moment for the change in perspective to come clear. The realisation lurched in his guts. It was Seb who knelt on the floor of his flat now. Yardley who dangled over the abyss.

Vaporous, the lad was, a veil through the radiance. Flesh and bone had long been eaten away, his mortal span done. Without access to his corpse, there was no way Yardley could change that. Even if he could, whatever he'd restore would only be an echo of his *shabab*, shuffling, cold and full of worms... No. The magician gazed up into Seb's soul, glittering, bright on the threshold. Released from the Province below.

Seb!

Yardley couldn't see the demon. But he could hear its laughter.

"Fuck me," Ormenus said. "Did you think to deceive the Author of Deception himself?"

The light was fading. The *khetem* waning. Its intervention was all too brief. Despite the heat of the wasteland, Yardley shivered. The laughter was coming from below him now. At his side, the relic slipped from his fingers, hitting the floor like a slammed coffin lid. He grimaced. The demon, a servant of the Scale of Six, was sinking its claws into his leg.

"Have it your way, magician. One soul weighs as much as another."

Yardley wanted to scream. Instead, he looked up. Seb grinned down at him through the light and the wind. As time spooled out like yarn, unwinding from a knot into countless futures, innumerable pasts, the magician found himself standing in the Scarab Club, Cairo, '82. A young man with a fez perched atop his impeccable hair was touching his elbow lightly at the bar. *Abracadabra* blared from the record player. Outside, the sands shifted and swirled.

Yardley clung on. In the weft of history, he downed his cocktail, shrugging off the young man's grip. As if he hadn't noticed him, he turned his back, eclipsing those dark and glittering eyes, and struck up a conversation with a woman in a white dress with gold earrings. In the past, he sensed the young man's presence slip away from him, seeking other prey.

In the present, he smiled up at Seb.

"Seb. I..."

But there could be no words between them now. There isn't a joy the world can give like that it takes away, Byron once wrote. Yardley knew the truth of that now. He closed his eyes. Let go of Seb's hand. Even as the sky grew black and the wind took him, howling in his ears, he smiled. He knew this place. He'd walked here for thirty odd years, through the shadows and the waste. It was the landscape of his own heart.

Ormenus, the Author of All Calamities, dragged him into Hell.

AUTHOR BIO

James Bennett is a British writer raised in Sussex and South Africa. His travels have furnished him with an abiding love of diverse cultures, history and mythology. His short fiction has appeared internationally and his debut novel 'Chasing Embers' was shortlisted for Best Newcomer at the British Fantasy Awards 2017. His latest fiction can be found in the well-received 'The Book of Queer Saints', BFS Horizons and The Dark magazine. 'The Dust of the Red Rose Knight' comes out in March 2023 and a short story collection 'Preaching to the Perverted' is set to follow next year from esteemed publisher Lethe Press.

James lives in Spain where he's currently working on a new novel.

Feel free to follow him on Twitter: @JamesBennettEsq

Afterword

Thank you for picking up this issue of *Tales From Between*. We hope you enjoyed it. If you would like to support us (and never miss a thing we publish) please consider joining us over on Patreon: patreon.com/TalesFromBetween

TWITTER: @from_between

INSTAGRAM: @tales_from_between

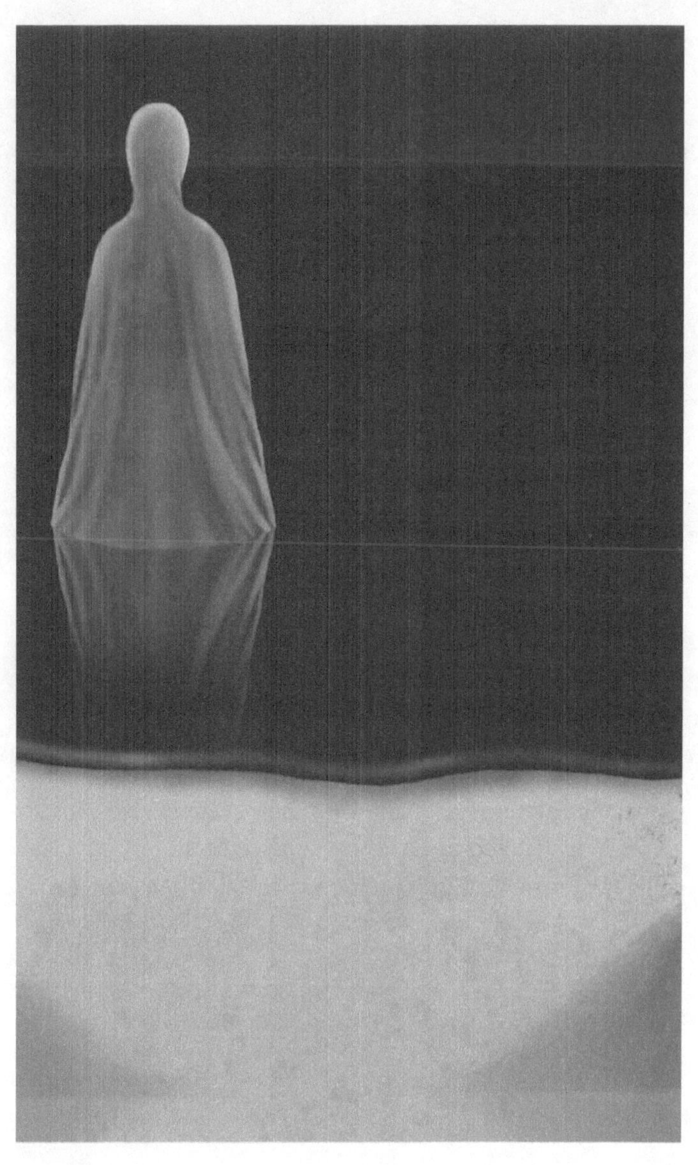

More To Read